Brilliance of the Moon

BATTLE FOR MARUYAMA

OTORI
CLAN

MARUYAMA
CLAN

SEISHUU
CLAN

SHIRAKAWA
CLAN

TOHAN
CLAN

TALES
OF THE

OTORI

EPISODE
5

Brilliance of the Moon

BATTLE FOR MARUYAMA

LIAN HEARN

PICADOR

First published 2004 by Riverhead Books,
a division of Penguin Group (USA) Inc.

First published in Great Britain in paperback 2006 by Picador
an imprint of Pan Macmillan Ltd
Pan Macmillan, 20 New Wharf Road, London N1 9RR
Basingstoke and Oxford
Associated companies throughout the world
www.panmacmillan.com

ISBN-13: 978-0-330-44699-0
ISBN-10: 0-330-44699-1

1 3 5 7 9 8 6 4 2

A CIP catalogue record for this book is available from
the British Library.

Printed and bound in Great Britain by
Mackays of Chatham, Kent

To B.

FOREWORD

These events took place in the months following the marriage of Otori Takeo and Shirakawa Kaede at the temple at Terayama. This marriage strengthened Kaede's resolve to inherit the domain of Maruyama and gave Takeo the resources he needed to carry out his work of revenge for his adopted father Shigeru and take his place as head of the Otori clan. However, it also enraged Arai Daiichi, the warlord who now controlled most of the Three Countries, and insulted the nobleman Lord Fujiwara, who considered Kaede betrothed to him.

The previous winter, Takeo, under the Tribe's sentence of death, had fled to Terayama, where the detailed records of the Tribe that Shigeru had compiled were given to him, along with the Otori sword Jato. On the way, his life was saved by the outcast Jo-An, one of the forbidden sect, the Hidden, who took him to a mountain shrine to hear the prophetic words of a holy woman.

Three bloods are mixed in you. You were born into the Hidden, but your life has been brought into the open and is no longer your own. Earth will deliver what heaven desires.

Your lands will stretch from sea to sea, but peace comes at the price of bloodshed. Five battles will buy you peace, four to win and one to lose. . . .

THE THREE COUNTRIES

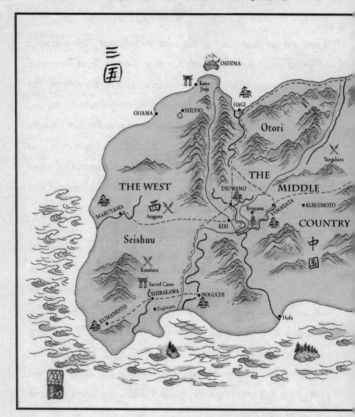

N 北

MATSUE

THE EAST

GAWA

東 Tohan

INUYAMA

● Hinode

 ● Mino

——————— *fief boundaries*

·········· *fief boundaries before Yaegahara*

— — — — — *high road*

⚔ *battlefields*

🏯 *castletown*

⛩ *shrine*

🏛 *temple*

CHARACTERS

The Clans

THE OTORI
(Middle Country; castletown: Hagi)

Otori Shigeru: rightful heir to the clan
Otori Takeshi: his younger brother, murdered by the Tohan
  clan **(d.)**
Otori Takeo: (born Tomasu) his adopted son
Otori Shigemori: Shigeru's father, killed at the battle of
  Yaegahara **(d.)**
Otori Ichiro: a distant relative, Shigeru and Takeo's teacher

Chiyo
Haruka: maids in the household

Shiro: a carpenter

Otori Shoichi: Shigeru's uncle, now lord of the clan
Otori Masahiro: Shoichi's younger brother
Otori Yoshitomi: Masahiro's son

Miyoshi Kahei: brothers, friends of Takeo
Miyoshi Gemba

Miyoshi Satoru: their father, captain of the guard in Hagi castle

Endo Chikara: a senior retainer

Terada Fumifusa: a pirate
Terada Fumio: his son, friend of Takeo

Ryoma: a fisherman, Masahiro's illegitimate son

THE TOHAN
(The East; castletown: Inuyama)

Iida Sadamu: lord of the clan
Iida Nariaki: Sadamu's cousin

Ando, Abe: Iida's retainers

Lord Noguchi: an ally
Lady Noguchi: his wife
Junko: a servant in Noguchi castle

THE SEISHUU
*(An alliance of several ancient families in the West;
main castletowns: Kumamoto and Maruyama)*

Arai Daiichi: a warlord

Niwa Satoru: a retainer
Akita Tsutomu: a retainer
Sonoda Mitsuru: Akita's nephew
Maruyama Naomi: head of the Maruyama domain,
    Shigeru's lover

Mariko: her daughter
Sachie: her maid

Sugita Haruki: a retainer
Sugita Hiroshi: his nephew
Sakai Masaki: Hiroshi's cousin

Lord Shirakawa
Kaede: Shirakawa's eldest daughter, Lady Maruyama's cousin
Ai, Hana: Shirakawa's daughters

Ayame
Manami
Akane: maids in the household

Amano Tenzo: a Shirakawa retainer

Shoji Kiyoshi: senior retainer to Lord Shirakawa

The Tribe

THE MUTO FAMILY

Muto Kenji: Takeo's teacher, the Master
Muto Shizuka: Kenji's niece, Arai's mistress, and Kaede's
    companion
Dr. Ishida: his physician
Zenko, Taku: her sons
Muto Seiko: Kenji's wife
Muto Yuki: their daughter
Muto Yuzuru: a cousin

Kana
Miyabi: maids

THE KIKUTA FAMILY

Kikuta Isamu: Takeo's real father (d.)
Kikuta Kotaro: his cousin, the Master
Kikuta Gosaburo: Kotaro's younger brother
Kikuta Akio: their nephew
Kikuta Hajime: a wrestler
Sadako: a maid

THE KURODA FAMILY

Kuroda Shintaro: a famous assassin
Kondo Kiichi
Imai Kazuo
Kudo Keiko

Others

Lord Fujiwara: a nobleman, exiled from the capital
Mamoru: his protégé and companion
Ono Rieko: his cousin
Murita: a retainer

Matsuda Shingen: the abbot at Terayama
Kubo Makoto: a monk, Takeo's closest friend

Jin-emon: a bandit

Jiro: a farmer's son

Jo-An: an outcast

Horses

Raku: gray with black mane and tail, Takeo's first horse, given
   by him to Kaede
Kyu: black, Shigeru's horse, disappeared in Inuyama
Aoi: black, half brother to Kyu
Ki: Amano's chestnut
Shun: Takeo's bay, a very clever horse

bold = main characters
(d.) = character died before the start of *Across the Nightingale Floor,
   Episode 1*

シテ　音づれの、稀なる中の秋風に、

地　憂さを知らする夕べかな。

シテ　遠里人の眺むらん、

地　誰が夜とし月はも訪ひし、

シテ　面白の折からや、増って、秋の夕っ方、

地　牝鹿の声に心ぞ澄む、見ぬ山風を

シテ　送り来て、梢はそれと葉を

地　散るや、空すさまじき、月影の、

シテ　軒の忍に映ろひて、

地　露のむすぶる夜すがらかな。

シテ　思ひを述ぶる身の、

地　宮漏高く立って、風北に巡り、

シテ　隣の砧緩く急いて、月西に流るる。

世阿弥作「砧」より

Others too, in far-flung villages,

Will no doubt be gazing at this moon

That never asks which watcher claims the night . . .

Loud on the unseen mountain wind,

A stag's cry quivers in the heart,

And somewhere a twig lets one leaf fall.

ZEAMI, *THE FULLING BLOCK (KINUTA)*

Brilliance of the Moon

BATTLE FOR MARUYAMA

EPISODE
5

· 1 ·

The feather lay in my palm. I held it carefully, aware of its age and its fragility. Yet its whiteness was still translucent, the vermilion tips of the pinions still brilliant.

"It came from a sacred bird, the *houou*," Matsuda Shingen, the abbot of the temple at Terayama, told me. "It appeared to your adopted father, Shigeru, when he was only fifteen, younger than you are now. Did he ever tell you this, Takeo?"

I shook my head. Matsuda and I were standing in his room at one end of the cloister around the main courtyard of the temple. From outside, drowning out the usual sounds of the temple, the chanting, and the bells, came the urgent noise of preparations, of many people coming and going. I could hear

Kaede, my wife, beyond the gates, talking to Amano Tenzo about the problems of keeping our army fed on the march. We were preparing to travel to Maruyama, the great domain in the West to which Kaede was the rightful heir, to claim it in her name—to fight for it if necessary. Since the end of winter, warriors had been making their way to Terayama to join me, and I now had close to a thousand men, billeted in the temple and in the surrounding villages, not counting the local farmers who also strongly supported my cause.

Amano was from Shirakawa, my wife's ancestral home, and the most trusted of her retainers, a great horseman and good with all animals. In the days that followed our marriage, Kaede and her woman, Manami, had shown considerable skill in handling and distributing food and equipment. They discussed everything with Amano and had him deliver their decisions to the men. That morning he was enumerating the oxcarts and packhorses we had at our disposal. I tried to stop listening, to concentrate on what Matsuda was telling me, but I was restless, eager to get moving.

"Be patient," Matsuda said mildly. "This will only take a minute. What do you know about the *houou*?"

I reluctantly pulled my attention back to the feather in

my palm and tried to recall what my former teacher, Ichiro, had taught me when I had been living in Lord Shigeru's house in Hagi. "It is the sacred bird of legend that appears in times of justice and peace. And it is written with the same character as the name of my clan, Otori."

"Correct," Matsuda said, smiling. "It does not often appear, justice and peace being something of a rarity in these times. But Shigeru saw it and I believe the vision inspired him in his pursuit of these virtues. I told him then that the feathers were tinged with blood, and indeed his blood, his death, still drive both you and me."

I looked more closely at the feather. It lay across the scar on my right palm where I had burned my hand a long time ago, in Mino, my birthplace, the day Shigeru had saved my life. My hand was also marked with the straight line of the Kikuta, the Tribe family to which I belonged, from which I had run away the previous winter. My inheritance, my past, and my future, all seemed to be there, held in the palm of my hand.

"Why do you show it to me now?"

"You will be leaving here soon. You have been with us all winter, studying and training to prepare yourself to fulfill Shigeru's last commands to you. I wanted you to share in his vision, to remember that his goal was justice, and yours must be too."

"I will never forget it," I promised. I bowed reverently over the feather, holding it gently in both hands, and offered it back to the abbot. He took it, bowed over it, and replaced it in the small lacquered box from which he had taken it. I said nothing, remembering all that Shigeru had done for me, and how much I still needed to accomplish for him.

"Ichiro told me about the *houou* when he was teaching me to write my name," I said finally. "When I saw him in Hagi last year he advised me to wait for him here, but I cannot wait much longer. We must leave for Maruyama within the week." I had been worrying about my old teacher since the snows had melted, for I knew that the Otori lords, Shigeru's uncles, were trying to take possession of my house and lands in Hagi and that Ichiro continued stubbornly to resist them.

I did not know it, but Ichiro was already dead. I had the news of it the next day. I was talking with Amano in the courtyard when I heard something from far below: shouts of anger, running feet, the trampling of hooves. The sound of horses plunging up the slope was unexpected and shocking. Usually no one came to the temple at Terayama on horseback. They either walked up the steep mountain path or, if unfit or very old, were carried by sturdy porters.

A few seconds later Amano heard it too. By then I was already running to the temple gates, calling to the guards.

Swiftly they set about closing the gates and barring them. Matsuda came hurrying across the courtyard. He was not wearing armor, but his sword was in his belt. Before we could speak to each other, a challenge came from the guardhouse.

"Who dares to ride to the temple gate? Dismount and approach this place of peace with respect!"

It was Kubo Makoto's voice. One of Terayama's young warrior monks, he had become, over the last few months, my closest friend. I ran to the wooden stockade and climbed the ladder to the guardhouse. Makoto gestured toward the spy hole. Through the chinks in the wood I could see four horsemen. They had been galloping up the hill; now they pulled their heaving, snorting mounts to a halt. They were fully armed, but the Otori crest was clearly visible on their helmets. For a moment I thought that they might be messengers from Ichiro. Then my eyes fell on the basket tied to the bow of one of the saddles. My heart turned to stone. I could guess, only too easily, what was inside such a container.

5

The horses were rearing and cavorting, not only from the exertion of the gallop, but also from alarm. Two of them were already bleeding from wounds to their hindquarters. A mob of angry men poured from the narrow path, armed with staves and sickles. I recognized some of them: They were farmers from the nearest village. The warrior at the rear made a rush at them, sword flailing, and they fell back slightly but did not disperse, maintaining their threatening stance in a tight half circle.

The leader of the horsemen flung a look of contempt at them and then called toward the gate in a loud voice.

"I am Fuwa Dosan of the Otori clan from Hagi. I bring a message from my lords Shoichi and Masahiro for the upstart who calls himself Otori Takeo."

Makoto called back, "If you are peaceful messengers, dismount and leave your swords. The gates will be opened."

I already knew what their message would be. I could feel blind fury building up behind my eyes.

"There's no need for that," Fuwa replied scornfully. "Our message is short. Tell the so-called Takeo that the Otori do not recognize his claims and that this is how they will deal with him and any who follow him."

The man alongside him dropped the reins on his horse's neck and opened the container. From it he took what I dreaded to see. Holding it by its topknot, he swung his arm and threw Ichiro's head over the wall into the temple grounds.

It fell with a slight thud onto the petaled grass of the garden.

I drew my sword, Jato, from my belt.

"Open the gate!" I shouted. "I am going out to them."

I leaped down the steps, Makoto behind me.

As the gates opened, the Otori warriors turned their horses and drove them at the wall of men around them, swords sweeping. I imagine they thought the farmers would not dare attack them. Even I was astonished at what happened next. Instead of parting to let them through, the men on foot hurled themselves at the horses. Two of the farmers died immediately, cut in half by the warriors' swords, but then the first horse came down, and its rider fell into the pack around him. The others met a similar fate. They had no chance to use their swordsmanship: They were dragged from their horses and beaten to death like dogs.

Makoto and I tried to restrain the farmers and eventually managed to drive them back from the bodies. We restored calm only by severing the warriors' heads and having them displayed on the temple gates. The unruly army threw insults at them for a while and then retired down the hill, promising in loud voices that if any other strangers dared approach the temple and insult Lord Otori Takeo, the Angel of Yamagata, they would be dealt with in the same way.

Makoto was shaking with rage—and some other emotion that he wanted to talk to me about—but I did not have the time then. I went back inside the walls. Kaede had brought white cloths and water in a wooden bowl. She was kneeling on the ground beneath the cherry trees, calmly washing the head. Its skin was blue-gray, the eyes half-closed, the neck not severed cleanly but hacked with several blows. Yet, she handled it gently, with loving care, as if it were a precious and beautiful object.

I knelt beside her, put out my hand, and touched the hair. It was streaked with gray, but the face in death looked younger than when I had last seen it, when Ichiro was alive in the house in Hagi, grieving and haunted by ghosts yet still willing to show me affection and guidance.

"Who is it?" Kaede said in a low voice.

"Ichiro. He was my teacher in Hagi. Shigeru's too."

My heart was too full to say more. I blinked away my tears. The memory of our last meeting rose in my mind. I wished I had said more to him, told him of my gratitude and my respect. I wondered how he had died, if his death had been humiliating and agonizing. I longed for the dead eyes to open, the bloodless lips to speak. How irretrievable the dead are, how completely they go from us! Even when their spirits return, they do not speak of their own deaths.

I was born and raised among the Hidden, who believe that only those who follow the commandments of the Secret God will meet again in the afterlife. Everyone else will be consumed in the fires of hell. I did not know if my adopted father Shigeru had been a believer, but he was familiar with all the teachings of the Hidden and spoke their prayers at the moment of his death, along with the name of the Enlightened One. Ichiro, his adviser and the steward of his household, had never given any such sign— in fact, rather the opposite: Ichiro had suspected from the start that Shigeru had rescued me from the warlord Iida Sadamu's persecution of the Hidden, and had watched me like a cormorant for anything that might give me away.

But I no longer followed the teachings of my childhood,

and I could not believe that a man of Ichiro's integrity and loyalty was in hell. Far stronger was my outrage at the injustice of this murder and my realization that I now had another death to avenge.

"They paid for it with their lives," Kaede said. "Why kill an old man and go to all that trouble to bring his head to you?" She washed away the last traces of blood and wrapped a clean white cloth around the head.

"I imagine the Otori lords want to draw me out," I replied. "They would prefer not to attack Terayama; they will run into Arai's soldiers if they do. They must hope to entice me over the border and meet me there." I longed for such a meeting, to punish them once and for all. The warriors' deaths had temporarily assuaged my fury, but I could feel it simmering in my heart. However, I had to be patient; my strategy was first to withdraw to Maruyama and build up my forces there. I would not be dissuaded from that.

I touched my brow to the grass, bidding my teacher good-bye. Manami came from the guest rooms and knelt a little way behind us.

"I've brought the box, lady," she whispered.

"Give it to me," Kaede replied. It was a small container

woven from willow twigs and strips of red-dyed leather. She took it and opened it. The smell of aloes rose from it. She put the white wrapped bundle inside and arranged the aloes round it. Then she placed the box on the ground in front of her, and the three of us bowed again before it.

A bush warbler called its spring song and a cuckoo responded from deep in the forest, the first I had heard that year.

We held the funeral rites the following day and buried the head next to Shigeru's grave. I made arrangements for another stone to be erected for Ichiro. I longed to know what had happened to the old woman, Chiyo, and the rest of the household at Hagi. I was tormented by the thought that the house no longer existed, that it would have been burned: the tea room, the upper room where we had so often sat looking out onto the garden, the nightingale floor, all destroyed, their song silenced forever. I wanted to rush to Hagi to claim my inheritance before it was taken from me. But I knew this was exactly what the Otori hoped I would do

Five farmers died outright and two died later from their wounds. We buried them in the temple graveyard. Two of the horses were badly hurt, and Amano had them killed mercifully, but the other two were unharmed; one I liked in particular, a handsome black stallion that reminded me of Shigeru's horse, Kyu, and could have been its half brother. At Makoto's insistence we buried the Otori warriors with full rites, too, praying that their ghosts, outraged at their ignoble deaths, would not linger to haunt us.

That evening the abbot came to the guest room and we talked until late into the night. Makoto and Miyoshi Kahei, one of my allies and friends from Hagi, were also with us; Kahei's younger brother Gemba had been sent to Maruyama to tell the domain's senior retainer, Sugita Haruki, of our imminent departure. Sugita had assured Kaede the previous winter of his support for her claim. Kaede did not stay with us—for various reasons, she and Makoto were not at ease in each other's presence and she avoided him as much as possible—but I told her beforehand to sit behind the screen so she could hear what was said. I wanted to know her opinion afterward. In the short time since our marriage I had come to talk to her as I had never talked to anyone in my life. I had been silent for so long, it seemed now I could not get enough of sharing my thoughts with her. I relied on her judgment and her wisdom.

"So now you are at war," the abbot said, "and your army has had its first skirmish."

"Hardly an army," Makoto said. "A rabble of farmers! How are you going to punish them?"

"What do you mean?" I replied.

"Farmers are not supposed to kill warriors," he said. "Anyone else in your situation would punish them with the utmost cruelty. They would be crucified, boiled in oil, flayed alive."

"They will be if the Otori get hold of them," Kahei muttered.

"They were fighting on my behalf," I said. Privately, I thought the warriors had deserved their shameful end, though I was sorry I had not killed them all myself. "I'm not going to punish them. I'm more concerned with how to protect them."

"You have let an ogre out," Makoto said. "Let's hope you can contain it."

The abbot smiled into his wine cup. Quite apart from his earlier comments on justice, he had been teaching me strategy all winter and, having heard my theories on the capture of Yamagata and other campaigns, knew how I felt about my farmers.

"The Otori seek to draw me out," I said to him, as I had said earlier to Kaede.

"Yes, you must resist the temptation," he replied. "Naturally your first instinct is for revenge, but even if you defeated their army in a confrontation, they would simply retreat to Hagi. A long siege would be a disaster. The city is virtually impregnable, and sooner or later you would have to deal with Arai's forces at your rear."

Arai Daiichi was the warlord from Kumamoto who had taken advantage of the overthrow of the Tohan to seize control of the Three Countries. I had enraged him by disappearing with the Tribe the previous year, and now my marriage to Kaede would certainly enrage him further. He had a huge army, and I did not want to be confronted by it before I had strengthened my own.

"Then we must go first to Maruyama, as planned. But if I leave the temple unprotected, you and the people of the district may be punished by the Otori."

"We can bring many people within the walls," the abbot said. "I think we have enough arms and supplies to hold the Otori off if they do attack. Personally, I don't think they will. Arai and his allies will not relinquish Yamagata without

14

a long struggle, and many among the Otori would be reluctant to destroy this place, which is sacred to the clan. Anyway they will be more concerned with pursuing you." He paused and then went on: "You can't fight a war without being prepared for sacrifice. Men will die in the battles you fight, and if you lose, many of them, including you yourself, may be put to death very painfully. The Otori do not recognize your adoption: They do not know your ancestry; as far as they are concerned you are an upstart, not one of their class. You cannot hold back from action because people will die as a result. Even your farmers know that. Seven of them died today, but those who survived are not sad. They are celebrating their victory over those who insulted you."

"I know that," I said, glancing at Makoto. His lips were pressed together tightly, and though his face showed no other expression, I felt his disapproval. I was aware yet again of my weaknesses as a commander. I was afraid both Makoto and Kahei, brought up in the warrior tradition, would come to despise me.

"We joined you by our own choice, Takeo," the abbot went on, "because of our loyalty to Shigeru and because we believe your cause is just."

I bowed my head, accepting the rebuke and vowing he would never have to speak to me in that vein again. "We will leave for Maruyama the day after tomorrow."

"Makoto will go with you," the abbot said. "As you know, he has made your cause his own."

Makoto's lips curved slightly as he nodded in agreement.

Later that night, around the second half of the hour of the Rat, when I was about to lie down beside Kaede, I heard voices outside, and a few moments later Manami called quietly to us to say that a monk had come with a message from the guardhouse.

"We have taken a prisoner," he said when I went to speak to him. "He was spotted skulking in the bushes beyond the gate. The guards pursued him and would have killed him on the spot, but he called your name and said he was your man."

"I'll come and talk to him," I said, taking up Jato, suspecting it could only be the outcast Jo-An. Jo-An had seen me at Yamagata when I had released his brother and other members of the Hidden into death. It was he who had given me the name of the Angel of Yamagata. Then he had saved my life on my desperate journey to Terayama in the winter. I had told him I would send for him in the spring and that he should wait until he heard from me, but he acted in unpredictable ways, usually in response to what he claimed was the voice of the Secret God.

It was a soft, warm night, the air already holding summer's humidity. In the cedars an owl was hooting. Jo-An lay on the ground just inside the gate. He'd been trussed up roughly: His legs were bent under him, his hands bound behind his back. His face was streaked with dirt and blood, his hair matted. He was moving his lips very slightly, praying soundlessly. Two monks were watching him from a careful distance, their faces twisted in contempt.

I called his name and his eyes opened. I saw relief shine in them. He tried to scrabble into a kneeling position and fell forward, unable to save himself with his hands. His face hit the dirt.

"Untie him," I said.

One of the monks said, "He is an outcast. We should not touch him."

"Who tied him up?"

"We did not realize then," the other said.

"You can cleanse yourselves later. This man saved my life. Untie him."

Reluctantly they went to Jo-An, lifted him up, and loosened the cords that bound him. He crawled forward and prostrated himself at my feet.

"Sit up, Jo-An," I said. "Why are you here? I said you were to come when I sent for you. You were lucky not to be killed, turning up here without warning, without permission."

The last time I'd seen him I'd been almost as shabbily dressed as he was, a fugitive, exhausted and starving. Now I was aware of the robe I wore, my hair dressed in the warrior style, the sword in my belt. I knew the sight of me talking to the outcast would shock the monks profoundly. Part of me was tempted to have him thrown out, to deny that there was any relationship between us, and to throw him from my life at the same time. If I so ordered the guards, they would kill him immediately with no second thought. Yet, I could not do it. He had saved my life; moreover, for the sake of the bond between us, both born into the Hidden, I had to treat him not as an outcast but as a man.

"No one will kill me until the Secret One calls me home," he muttered, raising his eyes and looking at me.

"Until that time, my life is yours." There was little light where we stood, just the lamp the monk had brought from the guardhouse and placed on the ground near us, but I could see Jo-An's eyes burning. I wondered, as I often had before, if he were not alive at all but a visitant from another world.

"What do you want?" I said.

"I have something to tell you. Very important. You'll be glad I came."

The monks had stepped back out of pollution's way but were still close enough to hear us.

"I need to talk to this man," I said. "Where should we go?"

They threw an anguished look at each other and the older man suggested, "Maybe the pavilion, in the garden?"

"You don't need to come with me."

"We should guard Lord Otori," the younger said.

"I'm in no danger from this man. Leave us alone. But tell Manami to bring water, some food, and tea."

They bowed and left. As they crossed the courtyard they started whispering to each other. I could hear every word. I sighed.

"Come with me," I said to Jo-An. He limped after me to the pavilion, which stood in the garden not far from the large pool. Its surface glittered in the starlight, and every now and then a fish leaped from the water, flopping back with a loud splash. Beyond the pool the grayish white stones of the graves loomed out of the darkness. The owl hooted again, closer this time.

"God told me to come to you," he said when we were settled on the wooden floor of the pavilion.

"You should not talk so openly of God," I chided him. "You are in a temple. The monks have no more love for the Hidden than the warriors."

"You are here," he muttered. "You are our hope and our protection."

"I'm just one person. I can't protect all of you from the way a whole country feels."

He was silent for a moment or two. Then he said, "The Secret One thinks about you all the time, even if you have forgotten him."

I did not want to listen to this sort of message.

"What do you have to tell me?" I said impatiently.

"The men you saw last year, the charcoal burners, were taking their god back to the mountain. I met them on the path. They told me the Otori armies are out, watching every road around Terayama and Yamagata. I went to look for myself. There are soldiers hidden everywhere. They will ambush you as soon as you leave. If you want to get out, you will have to fight your way through them."

His eyes were fixed on me, watching my reaction. I was cursing myself for having stayed so long at the temple. I'd been aware all along that speed and surprise were my main weapons. I should have left days before. I had been putting off leaving, waiting for Ichiro. Before my marriage I'd gone out night after night to check the roads around the temple for just such an eventuality. But since Kaede had joined me I could not tear myself away from her. Now I was trapped by my own vacillation and lack of vigilance.

"How many men would you say?"

"Five or six thousand," he replied.

I had barely a thousand.

"So you'll have to go over the mountain as you did in the winter. There's a track that goes west. No one's watching it, because there's still snow on the pass."

My mind was racing. I knew the path he meant. It went past the shrine where Makoto had planned to spend the winter before I stumbled in out of the snow on my flight to

Terayama. I'd explored it myself a few weeks earlier, turning back when the snow became too deep to wade through. I thought of my forces, men, horses, oxen: Oxen would never make it, but men and horses might. I would send them at night if possible, so the Otori would think we were still in the temple. . . . I would have to start at once, consult the abbot immediately.

My thoughts were interrupted by Manami and one of the manservants. The man was carrying a bowl of water. Manami brought a tray with a bowl of rice and vegetables and two cups of twig tea. She set the tray down on the floor, gazing at Jo-An with as much revulsion as if he were a viper. The man's reaction was equally horrified. I wondered briefly whether it would harm me to be seen associating with outcasts. I told them to leave us and they did so quickly, though I could hear Manami's disapproving muttering all the way back to the guesthouse.

Jo-An washed his hands and face, then joined his hands together to say the first prayer of the Hidden. Even as I found myself responding to the familiar words, a wave of irritation swept over me. He had risked his own life again to bring me this vital news, but I wished he showed more discretion, and my spirits sank at the thought of the liability he might become.

When he had finished eating I said, "You'd better leave. You have a long journey home."

He made no response, but sat, head turned slightly sideways, in the listening position I was by now familiar with.

"No," he said finally. "I am to go with you."

"It's impossible. I don't want you with me."

"God wants it," he said.

There was nothing I could do to argue him out of it, short of killing him or imprisoning him, and these seemed shabby rewards for his help to me.

"Very well," I said, "but you can't stay in the temple."

"No," he agreed docilely, "I have to fetch the others."

"What others, Jo-An?"

"The rest of us. The ones who came with me. You saw some of them."

I had seen these men at the tannery by the river where Jo-An worked, and I would never forget the way they had stared after me with burning eyes. I knew they looked to me for justice and protection. I remembered the feather: Justice was what Shigeru had desired. I also had to pursue it for the sake of his memory and for these living men.

Jo-An put his hands together again and gave thanks for the food.

A fish leaped in the silence.

"How many are there?" I asked.

"About thirty. They're hiding in the mountains. They've been crossing the border in ones and twos for the last weeks."

"Isn't the border guarded?"

"There've been skirmishes between the Otori and Arai's men. At the moment there's a standoff. The borders are all open. The Otori have made it clear they're not challenging Arai or hoping to retake Yamagata. They only want to eliminate you."

It seemed to be everyone's mission.

"Do the people support them?" I asked.

"Of course not!" he said almost impatiently. "You know who they support: the Angel of Yamagata. So do we all. Why else are we here?"

I was not sure I wanted their support, but I could not help but be impressed by their courage.

"Thank you," I said.

He grinned then, showing his missing teeth, reminding me of the torture he had already suffered because of me.

"We'll meet you on the other side of the mountain. You'll need us then, you'll see."

I had the guards open the gates and said good-bye to him. I watched his slight, twisted shape as he scuttled away into the darkness. From the forest a vixen screamed, a sound like a ghost in torment. I shivered. Jo-An seemed guided and sustained by some great supernatural power. Though I no longer believed in it, I feared its force like a superstitious child.

I went back to the guest house, my skin crawling. I removed my clothes and, despite the lateness of the hour, told Manami to take them away, wash and purify them, and then come to the bathhouse. She scrubbed me all over and I soaked in the hot water for ten or fifteen minutes. Putting on fresh clothes, I sent the servant to fetch Kahei and then to ask the abbot if we might speak with him. It was the first half of the Hour of the Ox.

I met Kahei in the passageway, told him briefly what had transpired, and went with him to the abbot's room, sending the servant to fetch Makoto from the temple, where he was keeping the night vigil. We came to the decision that we would move the entire army as soon as possible, apart from a small band of horsemen who would remain at Terayama for a day to fight as a rear guard.

Kahei and Makoto went immediately to the village beyond the gates to rouse Amano and the other men and start packing up food and equipment. The abbot ordered servants to inform the monks, reluctant to sound the temple bell at this hour of night in case we sent a warning to spies. I went to Kaede.

She was waiting for me, already in her sleeping robe, her hair loose down her back like a second robe, intensely black against the ivory material and her white skin. The sight of her, as always, took my breath away. Whatever happened to us, I would never forget this springtime we had had together. My life seemed full of undeserved blessings, but this was the greatest of them.

"Manami said an outcast came and you let him in and spoke with him." Her voice was as shocked as her woman's had been.

"Yes, he's called Jo-An. I met him in Yamagata." I undressed, put on my robe, and sat opposite her, knee to knee.

Her eyes searched my face. "You look exhausted. Come and lie down."

"I will; we must try and sleep for a few hours. We march

at first light. The Otori have surrounded the temple; we are going over the mountain."

"The outcast brought you this news?"

"He risked his life to do so."

"Why? How do you know him?"

"Do you remember the day we rode here with Lord Shigeru?" I said.

Kaede smiled. "I can never forget it."

"The night before, I climbed into the castle and put an end to the suffering of the prisoners hanging on the walls. They were Hidden: Have you heard of them?"

Kaede nodded. "Shizuka told me a little about them. They were tortured in the same way by the Noguchi."

"One of the men I killed was Jo-An's brother. Jo-An saw me as I came out of the moat and thought I was an angel."

"The Angel of Yamagata," Kaede said, slowly. "When we came back that night, the whole town was talking about it."

"Since then we have met again; our fates seem to be entwined in some way. Last year he helped me get here. I would have perished in the snow but for him. On the way he took me to see a holy woman, and she said certain things about my life."

I had told no one, not even Makoto, not even Matsuda, of the words of the prophetess, but now I wanted to share them with Kaede. I whispered some of them to her: that in me three bloods mingled, I was born into the Hidden but my life was no longer my own, that I was destined to rule in peace from sea to sea, when earth delivered what heaven desired. I had repeated these words over and over to myself, and as I've said before, sometimes I believed them and sometimes I did not. I told her that five battles would bring us peace, four to win and one to lose, but I did not tell her what the saint had predicted about my own son: that I would die at his hands. I told myself it was too terrible a burden to lay on her, but the truth was that I did not want to talk about another secret I had kept from her: that a girl from the Tribe, Muto Kenji's daughter, Yuki, was carrying my child.

"You were born into the Hidden?" she said carefully. "But the Tribe claimed you because of your father's blood. Shizuka tried to explain it to me."

"Muto Kenji revealed that my father was Kikuta, from the Tribe, when he first came to Shigeru's house. He did not know, though Shigeru did, that my father was also half Otori." I had already shown Kaede the records that confirmed this. Shigeru's father, Otori Shigemori, was my grandfather.

"And your mother?" she asked quietly. "If you feel able to tell me . . ."

"My mother was one of the Hidden. I was raised among them. My family were massacred in our village, Mino, by Iida's men, and they would have killed me then if Shigeru had not rescued me." I paused and then spoke of what I had hardly allowed myself to think about. "I had two sisters, little girls. I imagine they were also murdered. They were nine and seven years old."

"How terrible," Kaede said. "I am always afraid for my sisters. I hope we can send for them when we arrive at Maruyama. I hope they are safe now."

I was silent, thinking of Mino, where we had all felt so safe.

"How strange your life has been," Kaede went on. "When I first met you, I felt you hid everything. I watched you go away as if into a dark and secret place. I wanted to follow you there. I wanted to know everything about you."

"I will tell you everything. But let's lie down and rest."

Kaede pulled back the quilt and we lay down on the mattress. I took her in my arms, loosening both our robes so I could feel her skin against mine. She called to Manami to put out the lamps. The smell of smoke and oil lingered in the room after the woman's footsteps had died away.

I knew all the sounds of the temple at night by now: the periods of complete stillness, broken at regular intervals by the soft padding of feet as the monks rose in the darkness and went to pray, the low chanting, the sudden note of a bell. But tonight that regular and harmonious rhythm was disturbed, with sounds of people coming and going all night. I was restless, feeling I should be part of the preparations, yet reluctant to leave Kaede.

She whispered, "What does it mean, to be one of the Hidden?"

"I was raised with certain beliefs; most I don't hold anymore." As I said this I felt my neck tingle, as if a cold breath had passed over me. Was it really true that I had abandoned the beliefs of my childhood—ones that my family had died for rather than give up?

"It was said that when Iida punished Lord Shigeru, it was because he was one of the Hidden—and my kinswoman Lady Maruyama too," Kaede murmured.

"Shigeru never spoke of it to me. He knew their prayers and said them before he died, but his last word was the name of the Enlightened One." Until today, I had hardly thought of this moment. It had been obliterated by the horror of what had followed, and by my overwhelming grief. Today I had thought of it twice, and suddenly for the first time I put together the prophetess's words and Shigeru's. "It is all one," she had said. So Shigeru had believed this too. I heard again her wondering laughter and thought I saw him smile at me. I felt that something profound had suddenly been revealed to me, something I could never put into words. My heart seemed to miss a beat in astonishment. Into my silenced mind several images rushed at once: Shigeru's composure when he was about to die, the prophetess's compassion, my own sense of wonder and anticipation the first day I had come to Terayama, the red-tipped feather of the *houou* on my palm. I saw the truth that lay behind the teaching and the beliefs, saw how human striving muddied the clarity of life, saw with pity how we are all subject to desire and to death, the warrior as much as the outcast, the priest, the farmer, even the emperor himself. What name could I give to that clarity? Heaven? God? Fate? Or a myriad of names like the countless old spirits that men believed dwelled in this land? They were all faces of the faceless, expressions of that which cannot be expressed, parts of a truth but never the whole truth.

"And Lady Maruyama?" Kaede said, surprised by my long silence.

"I think she held strong beliefs, but I never spoke to her about them. When I first met her, she drew the sign on my hand."

"Show me," Kaede whispered, and I took her hand and traced the sign on her palm.

"Are the Hidden dangerous? Why does everyone hate them?"

"They're not dangerous. They are forbidden to take life, and so they do not defend themselves. They believe everyone is equal in the eyes of their God, and that he will judge everyone after death. Great lords like Iida hate this teaching. Most of the warrior class do. If everyone is equal and God watches everything, it must be wrong to treat the people so badly. Our world would be overthrown from the ground up if everyone thought like the Hidden."

"And you believe this?"

"I don't believe such a God exists, but I believe everyone should be treated as if they were equal. Outcasts, farmers, the Hidden, should all be protected against the cruelty and greed of the warrior class. And I want to use anyone who is prepared to help me. I don't care if they're farmers or outcasts. I'll take them all into my armies."

Kaede did not reply; I imagined these ideas seemed strange and repellent to her. I might no longer believe in the God of the Hidden, but I could not help the way their teachings had formed me. I thought of the farmers' action against the Otori warriors at the temple gates. I had approved of that, for I saw them as equals, but Makoto had been shocked and outraged. Was he right? Was I unchaining an ogre that I could never hope to control?

Kaede said quietly, "Do the Hidden believe women are equal to men?"

"In God's eyes they are. Usually the priests are men, but if there is no man of the right age, the older women become priestesses."

"Would you let me fight in your army?"

"As skillful as you are, if you were any other woman, I would be glad to have you fight alongside me as we did at Inuyama. But you are the heir to Maruyama. If you were to be killed in battle, our cause would be completely lost. Besides, I could not bear it."

I pulled Kaede close to me, burying my face in her hair. There was one other thing I had to speak to her about. It concerned another teaching of the Hidden, one that the warrior class find incomprehensible: that it is forbidden to take your own life. I whispered, "We have been safe here. Once we leave, everything will be different. I hope we can stay together, but there will be times when we will be separated. Many people want me dead, but it will not be until the prophecy is fulfilled and our peaceful country stretches from sea to sea. I want you to promise me that whatever happens, whatever you are told, you will not believe I am dead until you see it with your own eyes. Promise you will not take your own life until you see me dead."

"I promise it," she said quietly. "And you must do the same."

I made the same vow to her. When she was asleep, I lay in the dark and thought about what had been revealed to me. Whatever had been granted to me was not for my sake but for the sake of what I might achieve: a country of peace and justice where the *houou* would not only be seen but would build its nest and raise its young.

·2·

We slept a little. I woke while it was still dark to hear
from beyond the walls the steady tramping of men
and horses filing up the mountain track. I called to Manami
and then woke Kaede and told her to dress. I would come
back for her when it was time to leave. I also entrusted to
her the chest that contained Shigeru's records of the Tribe. I
felt I had to have these protected at all times, a safeguard for
my future against the death sentence that the Tribe had
issued against me and a possible guarantee of alliance with
Arai Daiichi, now the most powerful warlord in the Three
Countries.

The temple was already feverish with activity, the monks

preparing not for the dawn prayers but for a counterattack on the Otori forces and the possibility of a long siege. Torches sent flickering shadows over the grim faces of men preparing for war. I put on leather armor laced with red and gold. It was the first time I had worn it with a real purpose. It made me feel older, and I hoped it would give me confidence. I went to the gate to watch my men depart as day broke. Makoto and Kahei had already gone ahead with the vanguard. Plovers and pheasants were calling from the valley. Dew clung to the blades of bamboo grass and to the spring spiders' webs woven between them—webs that were quickly trampled underfoot.

When I returned, Kaede and Manami were both dressed in men's clothes for riding, Kaede wearing the armor, made originally for a page, that I had picked out for her. I had had a sword forged for her, and she wore this in her belt, along with a knife. We quickly ate a little cold food and then returned to where Amano was waiting with the horses.

The abbot was with him, in helmet and leather cuirass, his sword in his belt. I knelt before him to thank him for all he had done for me. He embraced me like a father.

"Send messengers from Maruyama," he said cheerfully. "You will be there before the new moon."

His confidence in me heartened me and gave me strength.

Kaede rode Raku, the gray horse with the black mane and tail that I had given her, and I rode the black stallion we had taken from the Otori warriors, which Amano had called Aoi. Manami and some of the other women who traveled with the army were lifted onto packhorses, Manami making sure the chest of records was strapped behind her. We joined the throng as it wound its way through the forest and up the steep mountain path that Makoto and I had descended the previous year in the first snow. The sky was aflame, the sun just beginning to touch the snowy peaks, turning them pink and gold. The air was cold enough to numb our cheeks and fingers.

I looked back once at the temple, at its broad sloping roofs emerging from the sea of new leaves like great ships. It looked eternally peaceful in the morning sun, with white doves fluttering round the eaves. I prayed it would be preserved just as it was at that moment, that it would not be burned or destroyed in the coming fight.

The red morning sky was true to its threat. Before long, heavy gray clouds moved in from the West, bringing first showers, then steady rain. As we climbed toward the pass, the rain turned to sleet. Men on horseback did better than the porters, who carried huge baskets on their backs; but as the snow underfoot became deeper, even the horses had a hard time of it. I'd imagined that going into battle would be a heroic affair, the conch shells sounding, the banners flying. I had not imagined it would be this grim slog against no human enemy, just the weather and the mountain, and the aching climb upward, always upward.

The horses balked finally and Amano and I dismounted to lead them. By the time we crossed the pass, we were soaked to the skin. There was no room on the narrow track to ride back or ahead to check on my army. As we wound downward I could see its snakelike shape, dark against the last traces of snow, a huge many-legged creature. Beyond the rocks and scree, now appearing as the rain melted the snow, stretched deep forests. If anyone lay in wait for us there, we would be completely at their mercy. But the forests were empty. The Otori were waiting for us on the other side of the mountain.

Once under cover of the trees, we caught up with Kahei where he had stopped to give the vanguard a rest. We now did the same, allowing the men to relieve themselves in small groups and then eat. The damp air filled with the acrid smell of their piss. We had been marching for five or six hours, but I was pleased to see warriors and farmers alike had held up well.

During our halt, the rain grew heavier. I was worried about Kaede, after her months of ill health, but even though she seemed very cold, she did not complain. She ate a little, but we had nothing warm and could not waste time making fires. Manami was uncharacteristically silent, watching Kaede closely and nervously starting at any sound. We pressed on as soon as possible. By my reckoning it was after noon, sometime between the Hour of the Goat and that of the Monkey. The slope became less steep and soon the track widened a little, enough so that I could ride along it. Leaving Kaede with Amano, I urged my horse on and cantered down the slope to the head of the army, where I found Makoto and Kahei.

Makoto, who knew the area better than any of us, told me there was a small town, Kibi, not far ahead, on the other side of the river, where we should stop overnight.

"Will it be defended?"

"If at all, only by a small garrison. There's no castle, and the town itself is barely fortified."

39

"Whose land is it?"

"Arai put one of his constables in," Kahei said. "The former lord and his sons sided with the Tohan at Kushimoto. They all died there. Some of the retainers joined Arai; the rest became masterless and took to the mountains as brigands."

"Send men ahead to say we require shelter for the night. Let them explain that we do not seek battle; we are only passing through. We'll see what the response is."

Kahei nodded, called to three of his men, and sent them on at a gallop while we continued more slowly. Barely an hour later they were back. The horses' flanks were heaving, covered in mud to the stifle, their nostrils red and flared.

"The river is in full flood and the bridge is down," their leader reported. "We tried to swim across, but the current is too strong. Even if we had made it, the foot soldiers and packhorses never would."

"What about roads along the river? Where's the next bridge?"

"The eastern road leads through the valley back to Yamagata, straight back to the Otori," Makoto said. "The southern one leads away from the river over the range toward Inuyama, but the pass will not be open at this time of year."

Unless we could cross the river, we were trapped.

"Ride forward with me," I said to Makoto. "Let's take a look for ourselves."

I told Kahei to bring the rest of the army forward slowly, except for a rear guard of one hundred men, who were to strike out to the East in case we were already being pursued by that route.

Makoto and I had hardly gone half a mile before I could hear it, the steady sullen groan of a river in flood. Swollen by the melting snow, as inexorable as the season, the spring river poured its yellow-green water across the landscape. As we rode out of the forest through the bamboo groves and into the reed beds, I thought we had come to the sea itself. Water stretched before us as far as the eye could see, dappled by rain, the same color as the sky. I must have gasped, because Makoto said, "It's not as bad as it looks. Most of it is irrigated fields."

I saw then the squared pattern of dikes and paths. The rice fields would be boggy but shallow; however, through the middle of them ran the river itself. It was about one hundred feet wide, and had risen over the protective dikes, making it at least twelve feet deep. I could see the remains of the wooden bridge: two piers just showing their dark tops against the swirling water. They looked unspeakably forlorn beneath the drifting rain, like all men's dreams and ambitions laid waste by nature and time.

I was gazing at the river, wondering if we could swim across, reconstruct the bridge, or what in heaven's name, when above the steady roar of the water I heard the sounds of human activity. Focusing my attention, I thought I could recognize voices, the chink of an ax, then unmistakably the sudden crash of falling timber.

To my right, upstream, the river curved away around a bend, the forest growing closer to the banks. I could see the remnants of what might have been a jetty or loading dock, presumably for taking lumber from the forest to the town. I turned my horse's head and at once began to ride through the fields toward the bend.

"What is it?" Makoto called, following me.

"There's someone there." I grabbed at Aoi's mane as he slipped and almost lost his footing.

"Come back!" he shouted. "It's not safe. You can't go alone."

I heard him unsling his bow and fit an arrow to the cord.

The horses plunged and splashed through the shallow water. Some memory was stringing itself together in my mind, of another river, impassable for different reasons. I knew what—whom—I would find.

Jo-An was there, half-naked, soaking wet, with his thirty or more outcasts. They had taken lumber from the jetty, where it had been stranded by the flood, and had felled more trees and cut enough reeds to build one of their floating bridges.

They stopped work when they saw me, and began to kneel in the mud. I thought I recognized some of them from the tannery. They were as thin and wretched as ever, and their eyes burned with the same hungry light. I tried to imagine what it had cost them to abscond with Jo-An out of their own territory, to break all the laws against the felling of trees, on the faint promise that I would bring justice and peace. I did not want to think about the ways they would be made to suffer if I failed them.

"Jo-An!" I called, and he came to the horse's side. It snorted at him and tried to rear, but he took the bridle and calmed it. "Tell them to keep working," I said, adding, "So I am even further in your debt."

"You owe me nothing," he replied. "You owe God everything."

Makoto rode up alongside, and I found myself hoping he had not heard Jo-An's words. Our horses touched noses and the black stallion squealed and tried to bite the other. Jo-An smacked it on the neck.

Makoto's glance fell on him. "Outcasts?" he said, disbelieving. "What are they doing here?"

"Saving our lives. They're building a floating bridge."

He pulled his horse back a few steps. Beneath his helmet I could see the curl of his lips. "No one will use it—" he began, but I cut him off.

"They will, because I command it. This is our only way of escape."

"We could fight our way back to the bridge at Yamagata."

"And lose all our advantage of speed? Anyway, we would be outnumbered five to one. And we'd have no retreat route. I won't do that. We'll cross the river by the bridge. Go back to the men and bring many of them to work with the outcasts. Let the rest prepare for the crossing."

"No one will cross this bridge if it is built by outcasts," he said, and something in his voice, as if he were speaking to a child, enraged me. It was the same feeling I'd had months ago when Shigeru's guards had let Kenji into the garden at Hagi, fooled by his tricks, unaware that he was a master assassin from the Tribe. I could only protect my men if they obeyed me. I forgot Makoto was older, wiser, and more experienced than I was. I let the fury sweep over me.

"Do as I command you at once. You must persuade them, or you'll answer to me for it. Let the warriors act as guards while the packhorses and foot soldiers cross. Bring bowmen to cover the bridge. We will cross before nightfall."

"Lord Otori." He bowed his head and his horse plunged and splashed away over the rice fields and up the slope beyond. I watched him disappear between the shafts of bamboo, then turned my attention to the outcasts' work.

They were lashing together the lumber they had collected and the trunks they had felled into rafts, each one supported on piles of reeds tied into bundles with cords plaited from tree bark and hemp. As each raft was finished they floated it out into the water and lashed it to the ones already moored in place. But the force of the current kept the rafts pushed into the bank.

"It needs to be anchored to the farther side," I said to Jo-An.

"Someone will swim across," he replied.

One of the younger men took a roll of cord, tied it round his waist, and plunged into the river. But the current was far too strong for him. We saw his arms flailing above the surface, then he disappeared under the yellow water. He was hauled back, half-drowned.

"Give the rope to me," I said.

Jo-An looked anxiously down the bank. "No, lord, wait," he begged me. "When the men come, one of them can swim across."

"When the men come, the bridge must be ready," I retorted. "Give me the rope."

Jo-An untied it from the young man, who was sitting up now, spitting out water, and handed it up to me. I made it fast around my waist and urged my horse forward. The rope slid over his haunches, making him leap; he was in the water almost before he realized it.

I shouted at him to encourage him, and he put one ear back to listen to me. For the first few paces his feet were on the bottom. Then the water came up to his shoulder and he began to swim. I tried to keep his head turned toward where I hoped we would land, but strong and willing as he was, the current was stronger, and we were carried by it downstream toward the remains of the old bridge.

I glanced toward it and did not like what I saw. The current was hurling branches and other debris against the piles, and if my horse were to be caught among them, he would panic and drown us both. I felt and feared the power of the river. So did he. Both ears lay flat against his head, and his eyes rolled. Luckily his terror gave him extra strength. He put in one great exertion, striking out with all four feet. We cleared the piles by a couple of arm spans and suddenly the current slackened. We were past the middle. A few moments later the horse found his footing and began to plunge up and down, taking huge steps to try and clear the water. He scrambled up onto firm ground and stood, head lowered, sides heaving, his former exuberance completely extinguished. I slipped from his back and patted his neck, telling him his father must have been a water spirit for him to swim so well. We were both saturated, more like fish or frogs than land animals.

I could feel the pull of the cord around my waist and dreaded it taking me back into the water. I half crawled, half scrambled to a small grove of trees at the edge of the river. They stood around a tiny shrine dedicated to the fox god, judging by the white statues, and were submerged to their lower branches by the flood. It lapped at the feet of the statues, making the foxes look as if they floated. I passed the cord around the trunk of the nearest tree, a small maple just beginning to burst into leaf, and started to haul on it. It was attached to a much stronger rope; I could feel its sodden weight as it came reluctantly up out of the river. Once I had enough length on it, I secured it to another, larger tree. It occurred to me that I was probably going to pollute the shrine in some way, but at that moment I did not care what god, spirit, or demon I offended as long as I got my men safely across the river.

All the time I was listening. Despite the rain I couldn't believe this place was as deserted as it seemed; it was at the site of a bridge on what appeared to be a well-used road. Through the hiss of the rain and the roar of the river I could hear the mewing of kites, the croaking of hundreds of frogs, enthusiastic about the wet, and crows calling harshly from the forest. But where were all the people?

Once the rope was secure, about ten of the outcasts crossed the river holding on to it. Far more skilled than I, they redid all my knots and set up a pulley system using the smooth branches of the maple. Slowly, laboriously, they hauled on the rafts, their chests heaving, their muscles standing out like cords. The river tore at the rafts, resenting their intrusion into its domain, but the men persisted and the rafts, made buoyant and stable by their reed mattresses, responded like oxen and came inch by inch toward us.

One side of the floating bridge was jammed by the current against the existing piles. Otherwise I think the river would have defeated us. I could see the bridge was close to being finished, but there was no sign of Makoto returning with the warriors. I had lost all sense of time, and the clouds were too low and dark to be able to discern the position of the sun, but I thought at least an hour must have passed. Had Makoto not been able to persuade them? Had they turned back to Yamagata as he had suggested? Closest friend or not, I would kill him with my own hands if they had. I strained my ears but could hear nothing except the river, the rain, and the frogs.

Beyond the shrine, where I stood, the road emerged from the water. I could see the mountains behind it, white mist hanging like streamers to their slopes. My horse was shivering. I thought I should move him around a little to keep him warm, since I had no idea how I would ever get him dry. I mounted and went a little way along the road, thinking also that I might get a better view across the river from the higher ground.

Not far along stood a kind of hovel built from wood and daub and roughly thatched with reeds. A wooden barrier had been placed across the road beside it. I wondered what it was: It did not look like an official fief border post and there did not seem to be any guards.

As I came closer I saw that several human heads were attached to the barrier, some freshly killed, others no more than skulls. I'd barely had time to feel revulsion when, from behind me, my ears caught the sound I'd been waiting for: the tramping of horses and men from the other side of the river. I looked back and saw through the rain the vanguard of my army emerging from the forest and splashing toward the bridge. I recognized Kahei by his helmet. He was riding in the front, Makoto alongside him.

My chest lightened with relief. I turned Aoi back; he saw the distant shapes of his fellows and gave a loud neigh. This was echoed at once by a tremendous shout from inside the hovel. The ground shook as the door was thrown open and the largest man I'd ever seen, larger even than the charcoal burners' giant, stepped out.

My first thought was that he was an ogre or a demon. He was nearly two arm spans tall and as broad as an ox; yet despite his bulk his head seemed far too large, as if the skull bone had never stopped growing. His hair was long and matted, he had a thick, wiry mustache and beard, and his eyes were not human-shaped but round like an animal's. He had only one ear, massive and pendulous. Where the other ear had been, a blue-gray scar gleamed through his hair. But his speech when he shouted at me was human enough.

"Hey!" he yelled in his enormous voice. "What d'you think y'doing on my road?"

"I am Otori Takeo," I replied. "I am bringing my army through. Clear the barrier!"

He laughed; it was like the sound of rocks crashing down the side of a mountain. "No one comes through here unless Jin-emon says they can. Go back and tell your army that!"

The rain was falling more heavily; the day was rapidly losing its light. I was exhausted, hungry, wet, and cold. "Clear the road," I shouted impatiently. "We are coming through."

He strode toward me without answering. He was carrying

a weapon, but he held it behind his back so I could not see clearly what it was. I heard the sound before I saw his arm move: a sort of metallic clink. With one hand I swung the horse's head around, with the other I drew Jato. Aoi heard the sound, too, and saw the giant's arm lunge outward. He shied sideways, and the ogre's stick and chain went past my ears, howling like a wolf.

The chain was weighted at one end and the stick to which the other end was attached had a sickle set in it. I'd never encountered such a weapon before, and had no idea how to fight him. The chain swung again, catching the horse round the right hind leg. Aoi screamed in pain and fear and lashed out. I kicked my feet from the stirrups, slid down on the opposite side from the ogre, and turned to face him. I'd obviously fallen in with a madman who was going to kill me if I did not kill him first.

He grinned at me. I must have looked to him no larger than the Peach Boy or some other tiny character from a folktale. I caught the beginning of movement in his muscle and split my image, throwing myself to the left. The chain went harmlessly through my second self. Jato leaped through the air between us and sank its blade into his lower arm, just above the wrist. Ordinarily it would have taken off the hand, but this adversary had bones of stone. I felt the reverberations up into my shoulder, and for a moment I feared my sword would lodge in his arm like an ax in a tree.

Jin-emon made a kind of creaking groan, not unlike the sound of the mountain when it freezes, and transferred the stick to his other hand. Blood was now oozing from his right hand, dark blackish-red in color, not splashing as you would expect. I went invisible for a moment as the chain howled again, briefly considered retreating to the river, wondering where on earth all my men were when I needed them. Then I saw an unprotected space and thrust Jato up into it and into the flesh that lay there. The wound left by my sword was huge, but again he hardly bled. A fresh wave of horror swept through me. I was fighting something nonhuman, supernatural. Did I have any chance of overcoming it?

On the next swing the chain wrapped itself round my sword. Giving a shout of triumph, Jin-emon yanked it from my hands. Jato flew through the air and landed several feet away from me. The ogre approached me, making sweeping movements with his arms, wise to my tricks now.

I stood still. I had my knife in my belt, but I did not

want to draw it, in case he swung his chain and ended my life there and then. I wanted this monster to look at me. He came up to me, seized me by the shoulders, and lifted me from the ground. I don't know what his plan was—maybe to tear out my throat with his huge teeth and drink my blood. I thought, *He is not my son, he cannot kill me,* and stared into his eyes. They had no more expression than a beast's, but as they met mine I saw them round with astonishment. I sensed behind them his dull malevolence, his brutal and pitiless nature. I realized the power that lay within me and let it stream from me. His eyes began to cloud. He gave a low moan and his grasp slackened as he wavered and crashed to the ground like a great tree under the woodsman's ax. I threw myself sideways, not wanting to end up pinned beneath him, and rolled to where Jato lay, making Aoi, who had been circling nervously around us, prance and rear again. Sword in hand, I ran back to where Jin-emon had fallen; he was snoring in the deep Kikuta sleep. I tried to raise the huge head to cut it off, but its weight was too great, and I did not want to risk damaging the blade of my sword. Instead, I thrust Jato into his throat and cut open the artery and windpipe. Even here the blood ran sluggishly.

His heels kicked, his back arched, but he did not waken. Eventually his breathing stopped.

I'd thought he was alone, but then a sound came from the hovel and I turned to see a much smaller man scuttling from the door. He shouted something incoherent, bounded across the dike behind the hut, and disappeared into the forest.

I shifted the barrier myself, gazing on the skulls and wondering whose they were. Two of the older ones fell while I was moving the wood, and insects crawled out from their eye sockets. I placed them in the grass and went back to my horse, chilled and nauseated. Aoi's leg was bruised and bleeding from where the chain had caught it, although it did not appear to be broken. He could walk, but he was very lame. I led him back to the river.

The encounter seemed like a bad dream, yet the more I pondered it, the better I felt. Jin-emon should have killed me—my severed head should now be on the barrier along with the others—but my Tribe powers had delivered me from him. It seemed to confirm the prophecy completely. If such an ogre could not kill me, who could? By the time I got back to the river, new energy was flowing through me. However, what I saw there transformed it into rage.

The bridge was in place, but only the outcasts were on the nearer side. The rest of my army were still on the other bank. The outcasts were huddled in that sullen way of theirs that I was beginning to understand as their reaction to the irrationality of the world's contempt for them.

Jo-An was sitting on his haunches, gazing gloomily at the swirling water. He stood when he saw me.

"They won't cross, lord. You'll have to go and order them."

"I will," I said, my anger mounting. "Take the horse, wash the wound, and walk him round so he doesn't chill."

Jo-An took the reins. "What happened?"

"I had an encounter with a demon," I replied shortly, and stepped onto the bridge.

The men waiting on the opposite side gave a shout when they saw me, but not one of them ventured onto the other end of the bridge. It was not easy to walk on—a swaying mass, partly submerged at times, pulled and rocked by the river. I half-ran, thinking as I did so of the nightingale floor that I had run across so lightly in Hagi. I prayed to Shigeru's spirit to be with me.

On the other side, Makoto dismounted and grasped my arm. "Where were you? We feared you were dead."

"I might well have been," I said in fury. "Where were you?" Before he could answer, Kahei rode up to us.

"What's the delay for?" I demanded. "Get the men moving."

Kahei hesitated. "They fear pollution from the outcasts."

"Get down," I said, and as he slid from his horse's back I let them both feel the full force of my rage. "Because of your stupidity I nearly died. If I give an order, it must be obeyed at once, no matter what you think of it. If that doesn't suit you, then ride back now, to Hagi, to the temple, to wherever, but out of my sight." I spoke in a low voice, not wanting the whole army to hear me, but I saw how my words shamed them. "Now send those with horses who want to swim into the water first. Move the packhorses onto the bridge while the rear is guarded, then the foot soldiers, no more than thirty at a time."

"Lord Otori," Kahei said. He leaped back in the saddle and galloped off down the line.

"Forgive me, Takeo," Makoto said quietly.

"Next time I'll kill you," I said. "Give me your horse."

I rode along the lines of waiting soldiers, repeating the command. "Don't be afraid of pollution," I told them. "I have already crossed the bridge. If there is any pollution, let it fall on me." I had moved into a state that was almost exalted. I did not think anything in heaven or on earth could harm me.

With a mighty shout, the first warrior rode into the water, and others streamed after him. The first horses were led onto the bridge, and to my relief it held them safely. Once the crossing was under way, I rode back along the line, issuing commands and reassuring the foot soldiers, until I came to where Kaede was waiting with Manami and the other women who accompanied us. Manami had brought rain umbrellas and they stood huddled beneath them. Amano held the horses alongside them. Kaede's face lit up when she saw me. Her hair was glistening with rain, and drops clung to her eyelashes.

I dismounted and gave the reins to Amano.

"What happened to Aoi?" he asked, recognizing this horse as Makoto's.

"He's hurt, I don't know how badly. He's on the other side of the river. We swam across." I wanted to tell Amano how brave the horse had been, but there was no time now.

"We are going to cross the river," I told the women. "The outcasts built a bridge."

Kaede said nothing, watching me, but Manami immediately opened her mouth to complain.

I put up my hand to silence her. "There is no alternative. You are to do what I say." I repeated what I had told the men: that any pollution would fall on me alone.

"Lord Otori," she muttered, giving the minimum bob of her head and glancing out of the corner of her eye. I resisted the urge to strike her, though I felt she deserved it.

"Am I to ride?" Kaede said.

"No, it's very unstable. Better to walk. I'll swim your horse across."

Amano would not hear of it. "There are plenty of grooms to do that," he said, looking at my soaked, muddy armor.

"Let one of them come with me now," I said. "He can take Raku and bring an extra horse for me. I must get back to the other side." I had not forgotten the man I'd seen scuttling away. If he had gone to alert others of our arrival, I wanted to be there to confront them.

"Bring Shun for Lord Otori," Amano shouted to one of the grooms. The man came up to us on a small bay horse and took Raku's reins. I said a brief farewell to Kaede, asking her to make sure the packhorse carrying the chest of records made the crossing safely, and mounted Makoto's horse again. We cantered back along the line of soldiers, which was now moving quite quickly onto the bridge. About two hundred were already across, and Kahei was organizing them into small groups, each with its own leader.

Makoto was waiting for me by the water's edge. I gave him his horse back and held Raku while he and the groom rode into the river. I watched the bay horse, Shun. He went fearlessly into the water, swimming strongly and calmly as if it were the sort of thing he did every day. The groom returned over the bridge and took Raku from me.

While they swam across, I joined the men on the floating bridge.

They scrambled across like the rats in Hagi Harbor, spending as little time on the soggy mass as possible. I imagined few of them knew how to swim. Some of them greeted me, and one or two touched me on the shoulder as if I would ward off evil and bring good luck. I encouraged them as much as I could, joking about the hot baths and excellent food we'd get in Maruyama. They seemed in good spirits, though we all knew that Maruyama lay a long way ahead.

On the other side I told the groom to wait with Raku for Kaede. I mounted Shun. He was on the small side, and not a handsome horse, but there was something about him I liked. Telling the warriors to follow, I rode ahead with Makoto. I particularly wanted bowmen with us, and two groups of thirty were ready. I told them to conceal themselves behind the dike and wait for my signal.

Jin-emon's body still lay by the barrier, and the whole place was silent, apparently deserted.

"Was this something to do with you?" Makoto said, looking with disgust at the huge body and the display of heads.

"I'll tell you later. He had a companion who got away. I suspect he'll be back with more men. Kahei said this area was full of bandits. The dead man must have been making people pay to use the bridge; if they refused, he took their heads."

Makoto dismounted to take a closer look. "Some of these are warriors," he said, "and young men too. We should take his head in payment." He drew his sword.

"Don't," I warned. "He has bones of granite. You'll damage the blade."

He gave me an incredulous look and did not say anything,

but in one swift movement slashed across the neck. His sword snapped with an almost human sound. There were gasps of astonishment and dread from the men around us. Makoto gazed at the broken blade in dismay, then looked shamefaced at me.

"Forgive me," he said again. "I should have listened to you."

My rage ignited. I drew my own sword, my vision turning red in the old, familiar way. How could I protect my men if they did not obey me? Makoto had ignored my advice in front of these soldiers. He deserved to die for it. I almost lost control and cut him down where he stood, but at that moment I heard the sound of horses' hooves in the distance, reminding me I had other, real enemies.

"He was a demon, less than human," I said to Makoto. "You had no way of knowing. You'll have to fight using your bow."

I made a sign to the men around us to be silent. They stood as if turned to stone; not even the horses moved. The rain had lessened to a fine drizzle. In the fading misty light we looked like an army of ghosts.

I listened to the bandits approach, splashing through the

wet landscape, and then they appeared out of the mist, over thirty horsemen and as many on foot. They were a motley, ragged band, some obviously masterless warriors with good horses and what had once been fine armor, others the riffraff left behind after ten years of war: escapees from harsh masters on estates or in silver mines; thieves; lunatics; murderers. I recognized the man who'd fled from the hovel; he was running at the stirrup of the leading horse. As the band came to a halt, throwing up mud and spray, he pointed to me and screamed, again something unintelligible.

The rider called, "Who is it who murdered our friend and companion, Jin-emon?"

I answered, "I am Otori Takeo. I am leading my men to Maruyama. Jin-emon attacked me for no reason. He paid for it. Let us through or you will pay the same price."

"Go back to where you came from," he replied with a snarl. "We hate the Otori here."

The men around him jeered. He spat on the ground and swung his sword above his head. I raised my hand in signal to the bowmen.

Immediately the sound of arrows filled the air; it is a fearful noise, the hiss and clack of the shafts, the dull thunk as they hit living flesh, the screams of the wounded. But I had no time to reflect on it then, for the leader urged his horse forward and galloped toward me, his sword arm stretched above his head.

His horse was bigger than Shun, and his reach longer than mine. Shun's ears were forward, his eyes calm. Just before the bandit struck, my horse made a leap to the side and turned almost in midair so I could slash my adversary from behind, opening up his neck and shoulder as he hit out vainly at where I had been.

He was no demon or ogre but all too human. His human blood spurted red. His horse galloped on while he swayed in the saddle, and then he fell suddenly sideways to the ground.

Shun, meanwhile, still completely calm, had spun back to meet the next attacker. This man had no helmet and Jato split his head in two, spattering blood, brains, and bone. The smell of blood was all around us, mixed with rain and mud. As more and more of our warriors came up to join the fray, the bandits were completely overwhelmed. Those who still lived tried to flee, but we rode after them and cut them down. Rage had been rising steadily in me all day and had been set alight by Makoto's disobedience; it found its release in this brief, bloody skirmish. I was furious at the delay that these lawless, foolish men had caused us, and I was deeply satisfied that they had all paid for it. It was not much of a battle, but we won it decisively, giving ourselves a taste of blood and victory.

We had three men dead and two others wounded. Later, four deaths by drowning were reported to me. One of Kahei's companions, Shibata from the Otori clan, knew a little about herbs and healing, and he cleaned and treated the wounds. Kahei rode ahead to the town to see what he could find in the way of shelter, at least for the women, and Makoto and I organized the rest of the force to move on more slowly. He took over command while I went back to the river where the last of the men were crossing the floating bridge.

Jo-An and his companions were still huddled by the water's edge. Jo-An stood and came to me. I had a moment's impulse to dismount and embrace him, but I did not act on it and the moment passed.

I said, "Thank you, and thanks to all your men. You saved us from disaster."

"Not one of them thanked us," he remarked, gesturing at the men filing past. "Lucky we work for God, not for them."

"You're coming with us, Jo-An?" I said. I did not want them

to return across the river, facing who knew what penalties for crossing the border, cutting down trees, helping an outlaw.

He nodded. He seemed exhausted, and I was filled with compunction. I did not want the outcasts with me—I feared the reaction of my warriors and knew the friction and grumbling their presence would cause—but I could not abandon them here.

"We must destroy the bridge," I said, "lest the Otori follow us over it."

He nodded again and called to the others. Wearily they got to their feet and began to dismantle the cords that held the rafts in place. I stopped some of the foot soldiers, farmers who had sickles and pruning knives, and ordered them to help the outcasts. Once the ropes were slashed, the rafts gave way. The current immediately swept them into the midstream, where the river set about completing their destruction.

I watched the muddy water for a moment, called my thanks again to the outcasts, and told them to keep up with the soldiers. Then I went to Kaede.

She was already mounted on Raku, in the shelter of the trees around the fox shrine. I noticed quickly that Manami was perched on the packhorse with the chest of records strapped behind her, and then I had eyes only for Kaede. Her face was pale, but she sat straight-backed on the little gray, watching the army file past with a slight smile on her lips. In this rough setting she, whom I had mainly seen restrained and subdued in elegant surroundings, looked happy.

As soon as I saw her, I was seized by the fiercest desire to hold her. I thought I would die if I did not sleep with her soon. I had not expected this and I was ashamed of how I felt. I thought I should have been concerned with her safety instead; moreover, I was the leader of an army: I had a thousand men to worry about. My aching desire for my wife embarrassed me and made me almost shy of her.

She saw me and rode toward me. The horses whickered at each other. Our knees touched. As our heads bent toward each other, I caught her jasmine scent.

"The road's clear now," I said. "We can ride on."

"Who were they?"

"Bandits, I suppose." I spoke briefly, not wanting to bring the blood and the dying into this place where Kaede was. "Kahei has gone ahead to find you somewhere to sleep tonight."

"I'll sleep outside if I can lie with you," she said in a low voice. "I have never felt freedom before, but today, on the journey, in the rain, in all its difficulties, I have felt free."

Our hands touched briefly, then I rode on with Amano, talking to him about Shun. My eyes were hot and I wanted to conceal my emotion.

"I've never ridden a horse like him before. It's as if he knows what I'm thinking."

Amano's eyes creased as he smiled. "I wondered if you would like him. Someone brought him to me a couple of weeks ago; my guess is he was either stolen or picked up after his owner was killed. I can't imagine anyone getting rid of him voluntarily. He's the smartest horse I've ever known. The black's more showy—good for making an impression—but I know which one I'd rather be on in a fight." He grinned at me. "Lord Otori is lucky with horses. Some people are. It's like a gift; good animals come to you."

"Let's hope it augurs well for the future," I replied.

We passed the hovel. The dead were laid out in rows along the dike. I was thinking that I should leave some men to burn or bury the corpses when there was a disturbance ahead, and one of Kahei's men came through on his horse, shouting at the soldiers to let him pass, calling my name.

"Lord Otori!" he said, reining in his horse just in front of us. "You're wanted up ahead. Some farmers have come to speak with you."

Ever since we'd crossed the river, I'd been wondering where the local people were. Even though the rice fields were flooded, there was no sign of their having been planted. Weeds choked the irrigation channels, and though in the distance I could see the steep thatched roofs of farmhouses, no smoke rose from them and there was no sign or sound of human activity. The landscape seemed cursed and empty. I imagined that Jin-emon and his band had intimidated, driven away, or murdered all the farmers and villagers. It seemed news of his death had traveled fast, and had now brought some of them out from hiding.

I cantered up through the file. The men called out to me, seeming cheerful; some were even singing. They were apparently unworried by the coming night, apparently had complete faith in my ability to find them food and shelter.

At the front of the army, Makoto had called a halt. A group of farmers were squatting on their heels in the mud. When I reached them and dismounted, they threw themselves forward.

Makoto said, "They've come to thank us. The bandits have been terrorizing this area for nearly twelve months. They've been unable to plant this spring for fear of them. The ogre killed many of their sons and brothers, and many of their women have been abducted."

"Sit up," I said to them. "I am Otori Takeo."

They sat up, but as soon as I spoke my name they bowed again. "Sit up," I repeated. "Jin-emon is dead." Down they went again. "You may do with his body what you wish. Retrieve your relatives' remains and bury them honorably." I paused. I wanted to ask them for food but feared they had so little, I would be condemning them to death by starvation once we had moved on.

The oldest among them, obviously the headman, spoke hesitantly. "Lord, what can we do for you? We would feed your men, but they are so many. . . ."

"Bury the dead and you owe us nothing," I replied. "But we must find shelter tonight. What can you tell us about the nearest town?"

"They will welcome you there," he said. "Kibi is an hour or so away on foot. We have a new lord, one of Lord Arai's men. He has sent warriors against the bandits many times this year, but they have always been defeated. The last time his two sons were killed by Jin-emon, as was my eldest son. This is his brother, Jiro. Take him with you, Lord Otori."

Jiro was a couple of years younger than I was, painfully thin, but with an intelligent face beneath the rain-streaked dirt.

"Come here, Jiro," I said to him, and he got to his feet and stood by the bay's head. It smelled him carefully as if inspecting him. "Do you like horses?"

He nodded, too overwhelmed by my addressing him directly to speak.

"If your father can spare you, you may come with me to Maruyama." I thought he could join Amano's grooms.

"We should press on now," Makoto said at my elbow.

"We have brought what we could," the farmer said, and made a gesture to the other men. They lowered their sacks and baskets from their shoulders and took out scant offerings of food: cakes made from millet, fern shoots and other wild greens cut from the mountain, a few tiny salted plums, and some withered chestnuts. I did not want to take them, but I felt to refuse would be to dishonor the farmers. I organized two soldiers to gather up the food and bring the sacks with them.

"Bid your father farewell," I said to Jiro, and saw the older man's face working suddenly to fight back tears. I regretted my offer to take the boy, not only because it was one more life to be responsible for, but also because I was depriving his father of his help in restoring the neglected fields.

"I'll send him back from the town."

"No!" both father and son exclaimed together, the boy's face reddening.

"Let him go with you," the father pleaded. "Our family used to be warriors. My grandparents took to farming rather than starve. If Jiro serves you, maybe he can become a warrior again and restore our family name."

"He would do better to stay here and restore the land," I replied. "But if it is truly what you want, he may come with us."

I sent the lad back to help Amano with the horses we had acquired from the bandits, telling him to come back to me when he was mounted. I was wondering what had happened to Aoi, whom I had not set eyes on since I'd left him with Jo-An; it seemed like days ago. Makoto and I rode knee by knee at the head of our tired but cheerful army.

"It's been a good day, a good start," he said. "You have done exceptionally well, despite my idiocy."

I remembered my earlier fury against him. It seemed to have evaporated completely now.

"Let's forget it. Would you describe that as a battle?"

"For unfledged men it was a battle," he replied. "And a victory. Since you won it, you can describe it however you like."

Three left to win, one to lose, I thought, and then almost immediately wondered if that was how a prophecy worked. Could I choose to apply it how it pleased me? I began to see what a powerful and dangerous thing it was: how it would influence my life whether I believed it or not. The words had been spoken to me, I had heard them, I would never be able to wipe them from my memory. Yet I could not quite commit myself to believing in them blindly.

Jiro came trotting back on Amano's own chestnut, Ki. "Lord Amano thought you should change horses, and sent you his. He doesn't think he can save the black horse. It needs to rest its leg, and won't be able to keep up. And no one here can afford to keep a creature that can't work."

I felt a moment of sorrow for the brave and beautiful horse. I patted Shun's neck. "I'm happy with this one."

Jiro slid from the chestnut's back and took Shun's reins. "Ki is better-looking," he remarked.

"You should make a good impression," Makoto said dryly to me.

We changed horses, the chestnut snorting through his nose and looking as fresh as if he'd just come from the meadow. Jiro swung himself up on the bay, but as soon as he touched the saddle, Shun put his head down and bucked, sending him flying through the air. The horse regarded the boy in the mud at his feet in surprise, almost as though thinking, *What's he doing down there?*

Makoto and I found it far funnier than it really was and roared with laughter. "Serves you right for being rude about him," Makoto said.

To his credit, Jiro laughed too. He got to his feet and apologized gravely to Shun, who then allowed him to mount without protest.

The boy lost some of his shyness after that and began to point out landmarks on the road, a mountain where goblins lived, a shrine whose water healed the deepest wounds, a roadside spring that had never dried up in a thousand years. I imagined that, like me, he'd spent most of his childhood running wild on the mountain.

"Can you read and write, Jiro?" I asked.

"A little," he replied.

"You'll have to study hard to become a warrior," Makoto said with a smile.

"Don't I just need to know how to fight? I've practiced with the wooden pole and the bow."

"You need to be educated as well, otherwise you'll end up no better than the bandits."

"Are you a great warrior, sir?" Makoto's teasing encouraged Jiro to become more familiar.

"Not at all! I'm a monk."

Jiro's face was a picture of amazement. "Forgive me for saying so, but you don't look like one!"

Makoto dropped the reins on his horse's neck and took off his helmet, showing his shaven head. He rubbed his scalp and hung the helmet on the saddlebow. "I'm relying on Lord Otori to avoid any more combat today!"

After nearly an hour we came to the town. The houses around it seemed to be inhabited and the fields looked better cared for, the dikes repaired and the rice seedlings planted out. In one or two of the larger houses, lamps were lit, casting their orange glow against torn screens. Others had fires burning in the earthen-floored kitchens; the smell of food wafting from them made our stomachs growl.

The town had once been fortified, but recent fighting had left the walls broken in many places, the gates and watchtowers destroyed by fire. The fine mist softened the harsh outlines of destruction. The river that we had crossed flowed along one side of the town; there was no sign of a bridge, but there had obviously once been a thriving boat trade, though now more boats seemed damaged than whole. The bridge where Jin-emon had set up his toll barrier had been this town's lifeline and he'd all but strangled it.

Kahei was waiting for us at the ruins of the main gateway. I told him to stay with the men while I went on into the town with Makoto and Jiro and a small guard.

He looked concerned. "Better that I go, in case there is some trap," he suggested, but I did not think this half-ruined place offered any danger, and I felt it wiser to ride up to Arai's constable as if I expected his friendship and cooperation. He would not refuse to help me to my face, whereas he might if he thought I had any fear of him.

As Kahei had said, there was no castle, but in the center of the town on a slight hill was a large wooden residence whose walls and gates had recently been repaired. The house itself looked run-down but relatively undamaged. As we approached, the gates were opened and a middle-aged man stepped out, followed by a small group of armed men.

I recognized him at once. He had been at Arai's side when the western army rode into Inuyama, and had accompanied Arai to Terayama. Indeed, he had been in the room when I had last seen Arai. Niwa, his name was, I recalled. Was it his sons who had been killed by Jin-emon? His face had aged and held fresh lines of grief.

I reined in the chestnut horse and spoke in a loud voice. "I am Otori Takeo, son of Shigeru, grandson of Shigemori. I intend no harm to you or your people. My wife Shirakawa Kaede and I are moving our army to her domain at Maruyama, and I ask for your help in providing food and lodging overnight."

"I remember you well," he said. "It's been a while since we last met. I am Niwa Junkei. I hold this land by order of Lord Arai. Are you now seeking an alliance with him?"

"That would give me the greatest pleasure," I said. "As soon as I have secured my wife's domain, I will go to Inuyama to wait on his lordship."

"Well, a lot seems to have changed in your life," he

replied. "I believe I am in your debt; news on the wind is that you killed Jin-emon and his bandits."

"It is true that Jin-emon and all his men are dead," I said. "We have brought back the warriors' heads for proper burial. I wish I had come earlier to spare you your grief."

He nodded, his lips compressed into a line so thin that it looked black, but he did not speak of his sons. "You must be my guests," he said, trying to infuse some energy into his tired voice. "You are very welcome. The clan hall is open to your men: It's been damaged, but the roof still stands. The rest may camp outside the town. We will provide such food as we can. Please bring your wife to my house; my women will look after her. You and your guard will of course also stay with me." He paused and then said bitterly, abandoning the formal words of courtesy, "I am aware that I am only offering you what you would otherwise take. Lord Arai's orders have always been to detain you. But I could not protect this district against a gang of bandits. What hope would I have against an army the size of yours?"

"I am grateful to you." I decided to ignore his tone, attributing it to grief. But I wondered at the scarcity of troops and supplies, the obvious weakness of the town, the impudence of the bandits. Arai must barely hold this country; the task of subduing the remnants of the Tohan must be taking up all his resources.

Niwa provided us with sacks of millet and rice, dried fish, and soybean paste, and these were distributed to the men along with the farmers' offerings. In their gratitude the townspeople welcomed the army and gave what food and shelter they could. Tents were erected, fires lit, horses fed and watered. I rode around the lines with Makoto, Amano, and Jiro, half-appalled at my own lack of knowledge and experience, half-amazed that in spite of it my men were settled down for the first night of our march. I spoke to the guards Kahei had set and then to Jo-An and the outcasts who had camped near them. An uneasy alliance seemed to have grown up between them.

I was inclined to watch all night too—I would hear an approaching army long before anyone else—but Makoto persuaded me to go back and rest for at least part of the night. Jiro led Shun and the chestnut away to Niwa's stables, and we went to the living quarters.

Kaede had already been escorted there and had been given a room with Niwa's wife and the other women of the household. I was longing to be alone with her, but I realized there would be little chance of it. She would be expected to sleep in the women's room, and I would be with Makoto and Kahei, several guards, and probably next door to Niwa and his guards too.

An old woman, who told us she had been Niwa's wife's wet nurse, led us to the guest room. It was spacious and well proportioned, but the mats were old and stained and the walls spotted with mildew. The screens were still open: On the evening breeze came the scent of blossom and freshly wet earth, but the garden was wild and untended.

"A bath is ready, lord," she said to me, and led me to the wooden bathhouse at the farther end of the veranda. I asked Makoto to keep guard and told the old woman to leave me alone. No one could have looked more harmless, but I was not taking any risks. I had absconded from the Tribe; I was under their sentence of death; I knew only too well how their assassins could appear under any guise.

She apologized that the water would not be very hot, and grumbled about the lack of firewood and food. It was in fact barely lukewarm, but the night was not cold, and just to scrub the mud and blood off my body was pleasure enough.

I eased myself into the tub, checking out the day's damage. I was not wounded, but I had bruises I had not noticed getting. My upper arms were marked by Jin-emon's steel hands—I remembered that all right—but there was a huge bruise on my thigh already turning black; I had no idea what had caused it. The wrist that Akio had bent backward so long ago at Inuyama and that I'd thought had healed was aching again, probably from the contact with Jin-emon's stone bones. I thought I would strap a leather band around it the following day. I let myself drift for a few moments and was on the point of falling asleep when I heard a woman's tread outside; the door slid open and Kaede stepped in.

I knew it was Kaede, by her walk, by her scent. She said, "I've brought lamps. The old woman said you must have sent her away because she was too ugly. She persuaded me to come instead."

The light in the bathhouse changed as she set the lamps on the floor. Then her hands were at the back of my neck, massaging away the stiffness.

"I apologized for your rudeness, but she said that where she grew up, the wife always looked after the husband in the bath, and that I should do the same for you."

"An excellent old custom," I said, trying not to groan aloud. Her hands moved to my shoulders. The overwhelming desire I'd felt for her came flooding back through me. Her hands left me for a moment and I heard the sigh of silk as she untied her sash and let it fall to the ground. She leaned forward to run her fingers across my temples and I felt her breasts brush the back of my neck.

I leaped from the bath and took her in my arms. She was as aroused as I was. I did not want to lay her down on the floor of the bathhouse. I lifted her and she wrapped her legs around me. As I moved into her I felt the rippling beginnings of her climax. Our bodies merged into one being, imitating our hearts. Afterward we did lie down, though the floor was wet and rough, clinging to each other for a long time.

When I spoke it was to apologize. I was ashamed again of the strength of my desire. She was my wife; I'd treated her like a prostitute. "Forgive me," I said. "I'm sorry."

"I wanted it so badly," Kaede said in a low voice. "I was afraid we would not be together tonight. I should ask your forgiveness. I seem to be shameless."

I pulled her close to me, burying my face in her hair. What I felt for her was like an enchantment. I was afraid of its power, but I could not resist it and it delighted me more than anything else in life.

"It's like a spell," Kaede said, as though she read my mind. "It's so strong I can't fight it. Is love always like this?"

"I don't know. I've never loved anyone but you."

"I am the same." When she stood her robe was soaked. She scooped water from the bath and washed herself. "Manami will have to find me a dry robe from somewhere." She sighed. "Now I suppose I have to go back to the women. I must try to talk to poor Lady Niwa, who is eaten up by grief. What will you talk about with her husband?"

"I'll find out what I can about Arai's movements and how many men and domains he controls."

"It's pitiful here," Kaede said. "Anyone could take over this place."

"Do you think we should?" The thought had already occurred to me when I'd heard Niwa's words at the gate. I also scooped water from the tub, washed myself, and dressed.

"Can we afford to leave a garrison here?"

"Not really. I think part of Arai's problem may be that he took too much land too fast. He has spread himself very thin."

"I agree," Kaede said, pulling her robe round her body and tying the sash. "We must consolidate our position at Maruyama and build up our supplies. If the land there is as neglected as it is here, and was at my home, we'll have trouble feeding our men once we get there. We need to be farmers before we can be warriors."

I gazed at her. Her hair was damp, her face soft from lovemaking. I had never seen a being as beautiful as she was, but beneath all that she had a mind like a sword. I found the combination and the fact that she was my wife unbearably erotic.

She slid the door open and stepped into her sandals. She dropped to her knees. "Good night, Lord Takeo," she said in a sweet, coy voice, quite unlike her own, rose lithely, and walked away, her hips swaying beneath the thin, wet robe.

Makoto sat outside, watching her, a strange look on his face, maybe disapproving, maybe jealous.

"Take a bath," I told him, "though the water's half-cold. Then we must join Niwa."

Kahei returned to eat with us. The old woman helped Niwa serve the food; I thought I caught a smirk on her face as she placed the tray before me, but I kept my eyes lowered.

By now I was so hungry, it was hard not to fall on the food and cram it in fistfuls into my mouth. There was little enough of it. Later the women came back with tea and wine and then left us. I envied them, for they would be sleeping close to Kaede.

The wine loosened Niwa's tongue, though it did not improve his mood; rather, it made him more melancholy and tearful. He had accepted the town from Arai, thinking it would make a home for his sons and grandsons. Now he had lost the first and would never see the second. His sons had not even, in his mind, died with honor on the battle-field, but had been murdered shamefully by a creature who was barely human.

"I don't understand how you overcame him," he said, sizing me up with a look that verged on scornful. "No offense, but both my sons were twice your size, older, more experienced." He drank deeply, then went on: "But then, I could never understand how you killed Iida, either. There was that rumor about you after you disappeared, of some strange blood in you that gave you special powers. Is it a sort of sorcery?"

I was aware of Kahei tensing beside me. Like any warrior he took immediate offense at the suggestion of sorcery. I did not think Niwa was being deliberately insulting; I thought he was too dulled by grief to know what he was saying. I made no reply. He continued to study me, but I did not meet his gaze. I was starting to long for sleep; my eyelids were quivering, my teeth aching.

"There were a lot of rumors," Niwa went on. "Your disappearance was a considerable blow to Arai. He took it very personally. He thought there was some conspiracy against him. He had a long-term mistress: Muto Shizuka. You know her?"

"She was a maid to my wife," I replied, not mentioning that she was also my cousin. "Lord Arai himself sent her."

"She turned out to be from the Tribe. Well, he'd known that all along, but he hadn't realized what it meant. When you went off, apparently to join the Tribe—or so everyone was saying—it brought a lot of things to a head."

He broke off, his gaze becoming more suspicious. "But you presumably know all this already."

"I heard that Lord Arai intended to move against the Tribe," I said carefully. "But I have not heard of the outcome."

"Not very successful. Some of his retainers—I was not among them—advised him to work with the Tribe as Iida did. Their opinion was that the best way to control them was to pay them. Arai didn't like that: He couldn't afford it for a start, and it's not in his nature. He wants things to be cut-and-dried and he can't stand to be made a fool of. He thought Muto Shizuka, the Tribe, even you, had hoodwinked him in some way."

"That was never my intention," I said. "But I can see how my actions must have looked to him. I owe him an apology. As soon as we are settled at Maruyama I will go to him. Is he at Inuyama now?"

"He spent the winter there. He intended to return to Kumamoto and mop up the last remnants of resistance there, move eastward to consolidate the former Noguchi lands, and then pursue his campaign against the Tribe, starting in Inuyama." He poured more wine for us all and gulped a cupful down. "But it's like trying to dig up a sweet potato: There's far more underground than you think, and no matter how carefully you try to lift it, pieces break off and begin to put out shoots again. I flushed out some members here; one of them ran the brewery, the other was a small-scale merchant and moneylender. But all I got were a couple of old men, figureheads, no more. They took poison before

I could get anything out of them. The rest disappeared."

He lifted the wine cup and stared morosely at it. "It's going to split Arai in two," he said finally. "He can handle the Tohan; they're a simple enemy, straightforward, and the heart mostly went out of them with Iida's death. But trying to eradicate this hidden enemy at the same time—he's set himself an impossible task, and he's running out of money and resources." He seemed to catch what he was saying and went on quickly: "Not that I'm disloyal to him. I gave him my allegiance and I'll stand by that. It's cost me my sons, though."

We all bowed our heads and murmured our sympathy.

Kahei said, "It's getting late. We should sleep a little if we are to march again at dawn."

"Of course." Niwa got clumsily to his feet and clapped his hands. After a few moments the old woman, lamp in hand, came to show us back to our room. The beds were already laid out on the floor. I went to the privy and then walked in the garden for a while to clear my head from the wine. The town was silent. It seemed I could hear my men breathing deeply in sleep. An owl hooted from the trees around the temple, and in the distance a dog barked. The gibbous moon of the fourth month was low in the sky; a few wisps of cloud drifted across it. The sky was misty, with only the brightest stars visible. I thought about all Niwa had told me. He was right: It was almost impossible to identify the network that the Tribe had set up across the Three Countries. But Shigeru had done so, and I had his records.

I went to the room. Makoto was already asleep. Kahei was talking to two of his men who had come to keep guard. He told me he had also put two men to watch the room where Kaede slept. I lay down, wished she were next to me, briefly considered sending for her, then fell into the deep river of sleep.

·3·

For the next few days our march to Maruyama continued without event. The news of Jin-emon's death and the defeat of his bandits had gone ahead of us and we were welcomed because of it. We moved quickly, with short nights and long days, making the most of the favorable weather before the full onset of the plum rains.

As we traveled, Kaede tried to explain to me the political background of the domain that was to become hers. Shigeru had already told me something of its history, but the tangled web of marriages; adoptions; deaths, that might have been murders; jealousy; and intrigue was mostly new to me. It made me marvel anew at the strength of Maruyama Naomi, the woman he had loved, who had been able to survive and rule in her own right. It made me regret her death, and his, all the more bitterly, and strengthened my resolve to continue their work of justice and peace.

"Lady Maruyama and I talked a little together on a journey like this," Kaede said. "But we were riding in the opposite direction, toward Tsuwano, where we met you. She told me women should hide their power and be carried in the palanquin lest the warlords and warriors crush them. But here I am riding beside you, on Raku, in freedom. I'll never go in a palanquin again."

It was a day of sun and showers, like the fox's wedding in the folktale. A sudden rainbow appeared against a dark gray cloud; the sun shone bravely for a few moments; rain fell silver. Then the clouds swept across the sky, sun and rainbow vanished, and the rain had a cold, harsh sting to it.

Lady Maruyama's marriage had been intended to improve relations between the Seishuu and the Tohan. Her husband was from the Tohan and was related to both the Iida and the Noguchi families. He was much older than she was, had been married before, and already had grown children. The wisdom of an alliance through such an encumbered marriage had been questioned at the time, not least by Naomi, who, although only sixteen, had been brought up in the Maruyama way to think and speak for herself. However, the clan desired the alliance, and so it was arranged. During Lady Maruyama's life her stepchildren had caused many problems. After her husband died they had contested the domain—unsuccessfully. Her husband's only daughter was the wife of a cousin of Iida Sadamu, Iida Nariaki—who, we learned on the way, had escaped the slaughter at Inuyama and had fled into the West, from where it seemed he now intended to make a new claim on the domain. The Seishuu clan lords were divided. Maruyama had always been inherited through the female line, but it was the last domain that clung to a tradition that affronted the warrior class. Nariaki had been adopted by his father-in-law before Lady Maruyama's marriage, and was considered by many to be legal heir to his wife's property.

Naomi had been fond of her husband and grieved genuinely when he died after four years, leaving her with a young daughter and a baby son. She was determined her daughter would inherit her estate. Her son died mysteriously, some said poisoned, and in the years that followed the battle of

Yaegahara, the widowed Naomi attracted the attention of Iida Sadamu himself.

"But by that time she had met Shigeru," I said, wishing I knew where and how. "And now you are her heir." Kaede's mother had been Lady Maruyama's cousin, and Kaede was the closest living relative to the former head of the clan, for Lady Maruyama's daughter Mariko had died with her mother in the river at Inuyama.

"If I am allowed to inherit," Kaede replied. "When her senior retainer, Sugita Haruki, came to me late last year, he swore the Maruyama clan would support me, but Nariaki may have already moved in."

"Then we will drive him out."

On the morning of the sixth day we came to the domain border. Kahei halted his men a few hundred paces before it, and I rode forward to join him.

"I was hoping my brother would have met us before now," he said quietly.

I had been hoping the same. Miyoshi Gemba had been sent to Maruyama before my marriage to Kaede to convey the news of our imminent arrival. But we had had heard nothing from him since. Apart from my concerns for his safety, I would have liked some information about the situation in the domain before we entered it, the whereabouts of Iida Nariaki, the feelings in the town toward us.

The barrier stood at a crossroads. The guard post was silent, the roads on all sides deserted. Amano took Jiro and they rode off to the south. When they reappeared, Amano was shouting.

"A large army has been through: There are many hoofprints and horse droppings."

"Heading into the domain?" I called.

"Yes!"

Kahei rode closer to the guard post and shouted, "Is anyone there? Lord Otori Takeo is bringing his wife, Lady Shirakawa Kaede, heir to Lady Maruyama Naomi, into her domain."

No answer came from the wooden building. A wisp of smoke rose from an unseen hearth. I could hear no sound, other than the army behind me, the stamping of restless horses, the breathing of a thousand men. My skin was tingling. I expected at any moment to hear the hiss and clack of arrows.

I rode Shun forward to join Kahei. "Let's take a look."

He glanced at me, but he'd given up trying to persuade me to stay behind. We dismounted, called to Jiro to hold the horses' reins, and drew our swords.

The barrier itself had been thrown down and crushed in the rush of men and horses that had trampled over it. A peculiar silence hung around the place. A bush warbler called from the forest, its song startlingly loud. The sky was partly covered with large gray clouds, but the rain had ceased again and the breeze from the south was mild.

I could smell blood and smoke on it. As we approached the guardhouse we saw the first of the bodies just inside the threshold. The man had fallen across the hearth and his clothes were smoldering. They would have burned if they had not been soaked with blood from where his belly had been slashed open. His hand still gripped his sword, but the blade was clean. Behind him lay two others, on their backs; their clothes were stained with their own last evacuations, but not with blood.

"They've been strangled," I said to Kahei. It chilled me, for only the Tribe use garrotes.

He nodded, turning one over to look at the crest on his back. "Maruyama."

"How long since they died?" I asked, looking round the room. Two of the men had been taken completely by surprise, the third stabbed before he could use his sword. I felt fury rise in me, the same fury I'd felt against the guards in Hagi when they'd let Kenji into the garden or when I'd slipped past them—fury at the dullness of ordinary men who were so easily outwitted by the Tribe. They'd been surprised while they'd been eating, killed by assassins before any of them could get away to carry a warning of the invading army.

Kahei picked up the teakettle from where it had been sent flying. "Barely warm."

"We must catch up with them before they reach the town."

"Let's get moving," Kahei said, his eyes bright with anticipation.

But as we turned to go I caught a fresh sound, coming from a small storeroom behind the main guard post. I made a sign to Kahei to keep silent and went to the door. Someone was behind it, trying to hold his breath but definitely breathing, and shivering, and letting the breath out in what was almost a sob.

I slid the door and entered in one movement. The room

was cluttered with bales of rice, wooden boards, weapons, farming implements.

"Who's there? Come out!"

There was a scuttling noise and a small figure burst out from behind the bales and tried to slide between my legs. I grabbed it, saw it was a boy of ten or eleven years, realized he held a knife, and wrenched his fingers apart until he cried out and dropped it.

He wriggled in my grasp, trying not to sob.

"Stand still! I'm not going to hurt you."

"Father! Father!" he called.

I pushed him in front of me into the guardroom. "Is one of these your father?"

His face had gone white, his breath came raggedly, and there were tears in his eyes, but he still struggled to control himself. There was no doubt he was a warrior's son. He looked at the man on the floor whom Kahei had pulled from the fire, took in the terrible wound and the sightless eyes, and nodded.

Then his face went green. I pulled him through the door so he could vomit outside.

There'd been a little tea left in the kettle. Kahei poured

it into one of the unbroken cups and gave it to the boy to drink.

"What happened?" I said.

His teeth were chattering, but he tried to speak normally, his voice coming out louder than he'd intended. "Two men came through the roof. They strangled Kitano and Tsuruta. Someone else slashed the tethers and panicked the horses. My father ran after them, and when he came back inside the men cut him open with their knives."

He fought back the sob. "I thought they'd gone," he said. "I couldn't see them! They came out of the air and cut him open."

"Where were you?"

"I was in the storeroom. I hid. I'm ashamed. I should have killed them!"

Kahei grinned at the fierce little face. "You did the right thing. Grow up and kill them, then!"

"Describe the men to me," I said.

"They wore dark clothes. They made no sound at all. And they did that trick so that you could not see them." He spat and added, "Sorcery!"

"And the army that came through?"

"Iida Nariaki of the Tohan, together with some Seishuu. I recognized their crests."

"How many?"

"Hundreds," he replied. "They took a long time to go past. But it's not so long since the last ones rode through. I was waiting until I thought they had all gone. I was about to come out when I heard you, so I stayed hidden."

"What's your name?"

"Sugita Hiroshi, son of Hikaru."

"You live in Maruyama?"

"Yes, my uncle Sugita Haruki is chief retainer to the Maruyama."

"You'd better come with us," I said. "Do you know who we are?"

"You are Otori," he said, smiling for the first time, a wan, feeble smile. "I can tell by your crests. I think you are the ones we have been waiting for."

"I am Otori Takeo and this is Miyoshi Kahei. My wife is Shirakawa Kaede, heir to this domain."

He dropped to his knees. "Lord Otori. Lord Miyoshi's

99

brother came to my uncle. They are preparing men because my uncle is sure Iida Nariaki will not let Lady Shirakawa inherit without a fight. He's right, isn't he?"

Kahei patted him on the shoulder. "Go and say good-bye to your father. And bring his sword. It must be yours now. When the battle is won we will bring him to Maruyama and bury him with honor."

This is the upbringing I should have had, I thought, watching Hiroshi come back holding the sword, which was almost as long as he was. My mother had told me not to tear the claws off crabs, not to hurt any living creature, but this child had been taught since birth to have no fear of death or cruelty. I knew Kahei approved of his courage: He had been raised in the same code. Well, if I did not have ruthlessness by now, after my training in the Tribe, I would never get it. I would have to pretend it.

"They drove off all our horses!" Hiroshi exclaimed as we walked past the empty stables. He was shaking again, but with rage, I thought, not fear.

"We'll get them back, and more," Kahei promised him. "You go with Jiro, and stay out of trouble."

"Take him back to the women and tell Manami to look

after him," I said to Jiro as I took Shun from him and remounted.

"I don't want to be looked after," the boy announced when Kahei lifted him onto the back of Jiro's horse. "I want to go into battle with you."

"Don't kill anyone by mistake with that sword," Kahei said, laughing. "We're your friends, remember!"

"The attack must have come as a complete surprise," I said to Makoto, after telling him briefly what we'd learned. "The guardhouse was hardly manned."

"Or maybe the Maruyama forces were expecting it and pulled back all their available men to ambush them or attack on more favorable ground," he replied. "Do you know the land between here and the town?"

"I've never been here."

"Has your wife?"

I shook my head.

"Then you'd better get that boy back. He may be our only guide."

Kahei shouted to Jiro, who had not gone far. Hiroshi was delighted to be brought back again, and he knew a surprising amount about the terrain and the fortification of the town. Maruyama was a hill castle; a sizable town lay on the slopes and at the foot of the rounded hill on which the castle was built. A small, fast-flowing river supplied the town with water and fed a network of canals, kept well stocked with fish; the castle had its own springs. The outer walls of the town had formerly been kept in good repair and could be defended indefinitely, but since Lady Maruyama's death and the confusion that had followed Iida's downfall, repairs had not been kept up and guards were few. In effect, the town was divided between those who supported Sugita and his championship of Kaede, and those who thought it more practical to bend before the wind of fate and accept the rule of Iida Nariaki and his wife, whose claim, they said, also had legitimacy.

"Where is your uncle now?" I asked Hiroshi.

"He has been waiting a little way from the town with all his men. He did not want to go too far from it, in case it was taken over behind his back. So I heard my father say."

"Will he retreat into the town?"

The boy's eyes narrowed in an adult way. "Only if he absolutely has to, and then he would have to fall back to the castle, for the town can no longer be defended. We are very short of food: Last year's storms destroyed much of the harvest, and the winter was unusually hard. We could not stand a long siege."

"Where would your uncle fight if he had the choice?"

"Not far from the town gate this road crosses a river, the Asagawa. There's a ford; it's almost always shallow, but sometimes there's a flash flood. To get to the ford, the road goes down into a steep ravine and then up again. Then there's a small plain with a favorable slope. My father taught me you could hold up an invading army there. And with enough men you could outflank them and box them in the ravine."

"Well spoken, Captain," Kahei said. "Remind me to take you with me on all my campaigns!"

"I only know this district," Hiroshi said, suddenly bashful. "But my father taught me that in war one must know the terrain above everything."

"He would be proud of you," I said. It seemed our best plan would be to press on and hope to trap the forces in front of us in the ravine. Even if Sugita had pulled back into the town, we could take the attacking army by surprise from behind.

I had one more question for the boy: "You said it's possible to outflank an army in the ravine. So there's another route between here and the plain?"

He nodded. "A few miles farther to the north there is another crossing. We rode that way a few days ago to come here. After a day of heavy rain there was a sudden flood through the ford. It takes a little longer, but not if you gallop."

"Can you show Lord Miyoshi the way?"

"Of course," he said, looking up at Kahei with eager eyes.

"Kahei, take your horsemen and ride with all speed that way. Hiroshi will show you where to find Sugita. Tell him we are coming and that he is to keep the enemy bottled up in the ravine. The foot soldiers and farmers will come with me."

"That's good," Hiroshi said approvingly. "The ford is full of boulders; the footing is not really favorable to war horses. And the Tohan will think you are weaker than you are and underestimate you. They won't expect farmers to fight."

I thought, *I should be taking lessons in strategy from him.*

Jiro said, "Am I to go with Lord Miyoshi too?"

"Yes, take Hiroshi on your horse, and keep an eye on him."

The horsemen rode away, the hoofs echoing across the broad valley.

"What hour is it?" I asked Makoto.

"About the second half of the Snake," he replied.

"Have the men eaten?"

"I gave orders to eat quickly while we were halted."

"Then we can move on right away. Start the men now; I'll ride back and tell the captains and my wife. I'll join you when I've spoken to them."

He turned his horse's head, but before he moved off he gazed briefly at the sky, the forest, and the valley.

"It's a beautiful day," he said quietly.

I knew what he meant: a good day to die. But neither he nor I was destined to die that day, though many others were.

I cantered back along the line of resting men, giving the orders to move on and telling their leaders our plan. They got to their feet eagerly, especially when I told them who our main enemy was; they shouted mightily at the prospect of punishing the Tohan for the defeat at Yaegahara, the loss of Yamagata, and the years of oppression.

Kaede and the other women were waiting in a small grove of trees, Amano as usual with them.

"We are going into battle," I said to Kaede. "Iida Nariaki's army crossed the border ahead of us. Kahei has ridden around the side of them, where we hope he will meet up with his brother and Sugita. Amano will take you into the forest, where you must stay until I come for you."

Amano bowed his head. Kaede looked as if she were going to speak, but then she, too, inclined her head. "May the All-Merciful One be with you," she whispered, her eyes on my face. She leaned forward slightly and said, "One day I will ride into battle beside you!"

"If I know you are safe, I can give all my concentration to the fight," I replied. "Besides, you must protect the records."

"A battlefield is no place for a woman!" Manami said, her face drawn with anxiety.

"No," Kaede replied, "I would only be in the way. But how I wish I had been born a man!"

Her fierceness made me laugh. "Tonight we will sleep in Maruyama!" I told her.

I kept the image of her vivid, courageous face in my mind all day. Before we left the temple, Kaede and Manami had made banners of the Otori heron, the white river of the Shirakawa, and the hill of the Maruyama, and we unfurled them now as we rode through the valley. Even though we were going into battle, I still checked out the state of the countryside. The fields looked fertile enough, and should already have been flooded and planted, but the dikes were broken and the channels clogged with weeds and mud.

Apart from the signs of neglect, the army ahead of us had stripped the land and farms of whatever they could find. Children cried by the roadside, houses burned, and here and there dead men lay, killed casually, for no reason, their bodies left where they'd fallen.

From time to time when we passed a farm or hamlet, the surviving men and boys came out to question us. Once they learned that we were pursuing the Tohan and that I would allow them to fight, they joined us eagerly, swelling our ranks by about a hundred.

About two hours later, when it was well past noon, maybe coming into the hour of the Goat, I heard from ahead the sounds I had been listening for: the clash of steel, the whinnying of horses, the shouts of battle, the cries of the wounded. I made a sign to Makoto and he gave the order to halt.

Shun stood still, ears pricked forward, listening as attentively as I did. He did not whinny in response, as though he knew the need for silence.

"Sugita must have met them here, as the boy said," Makoto

murmured. "But can Kahei have reached him already?"

"Whoever it is, it is a major battle," I replied.

The road ahead disappeared downhill into the ravine. The tops of the trees waved their new green leaves in the spring sunshine. The noise of battle was not so great that I could not also hear birdsong.

"The bannermen will ride forward with me," I said.

"You should not go ahead. Stay in the center, where it is safer. You will be too easy a target for bowmen."

"It is my war," I replied. "It's only right that I should be the first to engage in it." The words may have sounded calm and measured; in truth I was tense, anxious to begin the fight and anxious to end it.

"Yes, it is your war, and every one of us is in it because of you. All the more reason for us to try and preserve you!"

I turned my horse and faced the men. I felt a surge of regret for those who would die, but at least I had given them the chance to die like men, to fight for their land and families. I called to the bannermen and they rode forward, the banners streaming in the breeze. I looked at the white heron and prayed to Shigeru's spirit. I felt it possess me, sliding beneath my skin, aligning itself with my sinews and bones. I drew Jato and the blade flashed in the sun. The men responded with shouts and cheers.

I turned Shun and put him into a canter. He went forward calmly and eagerly, as though we were riding together through a meadow. The horse to my left was overexcited, pulling against the bit and trying to buck. I could feel all the muscular tension in the rider's body as he controlled the horse with one hand while keeping the banner erect in the other.

The road darkened as it descended between the trees. The surface worsened, as Hiroshi had predicted, the soft, muddy sand giving way to rocks, then boulders, with many potholes gouged out by the recent floods. The road itself would have turned into a river every time it rained.

We slowed to a trot. Above all the sounds of battle I could hear the real river. Ahead of us a bright gap in the foliage showed where the road emerged from under the trees to run along its bank for a few hundred feet before the ford. Silhouetted against the brightness were dark shapes, like the shadows against paper screens that amuse children, writhing and clashing in the contortions of slaughter.

I had thought to use bowmen first, but as soon as I saw

the conflict ahead I realized they would kill as many allies as enemies. Sugita's men had driven the invading army back from the plain and were pushing them foot by foot along the river. Even as we approached, some were trying to break ranks and flee; they saw us and ran back in the other direction, shouting to alert their commanders.

Makoto had raised the conch shell and now blew into it, its haunting, eerie note echoing from the wall of the ravine on the far side of the river. Then the echo itself was echoed as a reply came from way ahead, too far away for us to see the man blowing it. There was a moment of stillness, the moment before the wave breaks, and then we were among them and the fight had begun.

Only the chroniclers writing afterward can tell you what happens in battle, and then they usually tell only the tale of the victor. There is no way of knowing when you are locked in the midst of it which way the fighting is going. Even if you could see it from above, with eagle's eyes, all you would see would be a quilt of pulsating color, crests and banners, blood and steel—beautiful and nightmarish. All men on the battle-field go mad: How else could we do the things we do and bear to see the things we see?

I realized immediately that our skirmish with the bandits had been nothing. These were the hardened troops of the Tohan and the Seishuu, well armed, ferocious, cunning. They saw the heron crest and knew at once who was at their rear. To revenge Iida Sadamu by killing me was the instant goal of half their army. Makoto had been being sensible when he'd suggested I stay protected in the center. I'd fought off three warriors, saved from the third only by Shun's sense of timing, before my friend caught up with me. Wielding his staff like a lance, he caught a fourth man under the chin, knocking him from the saddle. One of our farmers leaped on the fallen warrior and severed his head with his sickle.

I urged Shun forward. He seemed instinctively to find a path through the crush, always turning at the right moment to give me the advantage. And Jato leaped in my hand, as Shigeru had once said it would, until it streamed with blood from the point to the hilt.

There was a thick knot of men around Makoto and me as we fought side by side, and I became aware of another similar cluster ahead. I could see the Tohan banner fluttering above it. The two clusters surged and swirled as men rose and fell around them, until they were so close I could see my counterpart in the center of the other.

I felt a rush of recognition. This man wore black armor with a horned helmet, the same as Iida Sadamu had worn when I had looked up at him from beneath his horse's feet in Mino. Across his breast gleamed a string of gold prayer beads. Our eyes met above the sea of struggling men, and Nariaki gave a shout of rage. Wrenching at his horse's head and urging it forward, he broke through the protective circle around him and rode at me.

"Otori Takeo is mine!" he yelled. "Let no one touch him but me!" As he repeated this over and over again, the men attacking me fell back a little and we found ourselves face to face a few paces apart.

I make it sound as if there was time to think it all through, but in reality there was none. These scenes return to me in flashes. He was in front of me; he shouted again insultingly, but I barely heard the words. He dropped the reins on his horse's neck and lifted his sword with both hands. His horse was bigger than Shun, and he, like Iida, much larger than I. I was watching the sword for the moment it began to move, and Shun was watching it too.

The blade flashed. Shun jumped sideways and the sword hit only air. The impetus of the huge blow dislodged the rider momentarily. As he fell awkwardly against his horse's neck, it bucked, enough to unseat him further. He had to either fall or drop his sword. Sliding his feet free of the stirrups, he held the horse's mane with one hand and with surprising agility swung himself to the ground. He fell onto his knees but still held the sword. Then he leaped to his feet and in the same movement rushed at me with a stroke that would have taken off my leg, if Shun had stood still long enough for it to connect.

My men pressed forward and could easily have overcome him.

"Stay back!" I shouted. I was determined now to kill him myself. I was possessed by fury like nothing I had ever known, as different from the cold murders of the Tribe as day is from night. I let the reins fall and leaped from Shun's back. I heard him snort behind me and knew he would stand as still as a rock until I needed him again.

I stood facing Iida's cousin as I'd wished I'd faced Iida himself. I knew Nariaki despised me, and with reason: I did not have his training or his skills, but in his scorn I saw his weakness. He rushed forward, the sword whirling: His plan was to try to cut me down with his longer reach. I suddenly saw myself in the hall at Terayama, practicing with Matsuda. I saw Kaede's image as I had seen it then; she was my life and my strength. *Tonight we will sleep in Maruyama*, I promised her again, and the same move came to me.

Black blood, I thought; maybe I even shouted it aloud to Nariaki. *You have it and I have it. We are of the same class.* I felt Shigeru's hand within my own. And then Jato bit home and Iida Nariaki's red blood was spraying my face.

As he fell forward onto his knees Jato struck again, and his head bounced at my feet, his eyes still full of fury, his lips snarling.

That scene remains engraved in my memory, but little else does. There was no time to feel fear, no time to think at all. The moves I'd been taught by Shigeru and by Matsuda came to my sword through my arm but not by my conscious will. Once Nariaki was dead, I turned to Shun. Blinking the sweat from my eyes, I saw Jo-An at his head; the outcast held my enemy's horse too.

"Get them out of the way," I shouted. Hiroshi had been right about the terrain. As the Tohan and Seishuu troops were driven back and we advanced, the crush intensified. Terrified horses stumbled in holes, breaking their legs, or were forced up against boulders, unable to go forward or back, panicking.

Jo-An scrambled like a monkey onto Shun's back and forced his way through the milling men. From time to time I was aware of him, moving through the fray, taking riderless, panic-stricken animals to the forest. As he'd said, there are many tasks in a battle besides killing.

Soon I could see the Otori and Maruyama banners ahead of us, and I saw the Miyoshi crest too. The army between us was trapped. They continued to fight savagely, but they had no way out and no hope.

I don't think one of them escaped alive. The river foamed red with their blood. After it was all over and silence had descended, the outcasts took care of the bodies and laid them out in rows. When we met up with Sugita we walked along the lines of the dead, and he was able to identify many of them. Jo-An and his men had already taken charge of dozens of horses. Now they stripped the dead of their weapons and armor and arranged to burn the corpses.

The day had passed without my noticing time. It must

have been the Hour of the Dog; the battle had lasted five or six hours. Our armies had been roughly equal: a little under two thousand men on each side. But the Tohan had lost all of theirs, while we had less than a hundred dead and two hundred wounded.

Jo-An brought Shun back to me and I rode with Sugita into the forest where Kaede had been waiting. Manami had managed to set up camp with her usual efficiency and had lit a fire and boiled water. Kaede knelt on a carpet beneath the trees. We could see her figure through the silver-gray trunks of the beeches, cloaked by her hair, her back straight. As we drew nearer I saw that her eyes were closed.

Manami came to meet us, her eyes bright and red-rimmed. "She has been praying," she whispered. "She has sat like that for hours."

I dismounted and called her name. Kaede opened her eyes and joy and relief leaped into her face. She bowed her head to the ground, her lips moving in silent thanks. I knelt before her and Sugita did likewise.

"We have won a great victory," he said. "Iida Nariaki is dead, and nothing now will stop you from taking possession of your domain at Maruyama."

"I am immensely grateful to you for your loyalty and courage," she said to him, and then turned to me.

"Are you hurt?"

"I don't think so." The frenzy of battle was fading and I was aching all over. My ears were ringing, and the smell of blood and death that clung to me was nauseating me. Kaede looked unattainably clean and pure.

"I prayed for your safety," she said, her voice low. Sugita's presence made us awkward with each other.

"Take some tea," Manami urged us. I realized my mouth was completely dry, my lips caked with blood.

"We are so dirty . . ." I began, but she put the cup in my hand and I drank it gratefully.

It was past sunset and the evening light was clear and tinged with blue. The wind had dropped and birds were singing their last songs of the day. I heard a rustling in the grass and looked up to see a hare cross the clearing in the distance. I drank the tea and looked at the hare. It gazed back at me with its large, wild eyes for many moments before it bounded away. The tea's taste was smoky and bitter.

Two battles lay behind us, three ahead, if the prophecy was to be believed: *Two now to win and one to lose.*

·4·

One month earlier, after Shirakawa Kaede had left with the Miyoshi brothers to go to the temple guest house at Terayama, Muto Shizuka had set out for the secret village of her Tribe family, hidden in the mountains on the far side of Yamagata. Kaede had wept when they said farewell to each other, had pressed money on Shizuka and insisted she take one of the packhorses and send it back when she could, but Shizuka knew she would be quickly forgotten once Kaede was with Takeo.

Shizuka was deeply uneasy about leaving Kaede and about the impetuous decision to marry Takeo. She rode silently, brooding on the madness of love and the disaster the marriage would be to them. She had no doubt they would marry: Now that fate had brought them together again, nothing would stop them. But she feared for them once Arai heard the news. And when her thoughts turned to Lord Fujiwara, a chill came over her despite the spring sunshine. She knew he could only be insulted and outraged, and she dreaded what he might do in revenge.

Kondo rode with her, his mood no better than hers. He seemed distressed and annoyed at being dismissed so suddenly. Several times he said, "She could have trusted me! After all I've done for her! I swore allegiance to her, after all. I would never do anything to harm her."

Kaede's spell has fallen on him too, Shizuka thought. *He's been flattered by her reliance on him. She turned to him so often; now she will turn to Takeo.*

"It was Takeo's order that we leave," she told him. "He is right. He cannot trust any one of us."

"What a mess," Kondo said gloomily. "Where shall I go now, I wonder. I liked it with Lady Shirakawa. The place suited me." He threw his head back and sniffed.

"The Muto family may have new instructions for both of us," Shizuka replied shortly.

"I'm getting on," he grumbled. "I wouldn't mind settling down. I'll make way for the next generation. If only there were more of them!"

He turned his head and gave her his ironic smile. There was something in his look that unsettled her, some warmth behind the irony. In his guarded way he was making some kind of advance to her. Ever since he'd saved her life on the road to Shirakawa the previous year, a tension had existed between them. She was grateful to him and had at one time thought she might sleep with him, but then the affair had begun with Dr. Ishida, Lord Fujiwara's physician, and she had wanted no one but him.

Though, she thought ruefully, that was hardly being practical. Kaede's marriage to Takeo would effectively remove her from Ishida forever. She had no idea how she could ever meet the doctor again. His farewells had been warm; he had pressed her to return as soon as possible, had even gone so far as to say he would miss her. But how could she return to him if she was no longer in Kaede's service and part of her household? Their affair had been conducted with great secrecy thus far, but if Fujiwara were to hear of it, she feared for the physician's safety.

I am as bad as Kaede, she thought. *Truly you never reach the age when you escape being scorched by love.*

They passed through Yamagata and traveled another twenty miles to a village where they stayed the night. Kondo knew the innkeeper; they might even have been related, though Shizuka did not care enough to find out. As she feared, he made it clear that he wanted to sleep with her, and she saw the disappointment in his eyes when she pleaded exhaustion, but he did not press her or force her as he might have done. She felt grateful and then annoyed with herself for so feeling.

However, the next morning, after they had left the horses at the inn and begun the steep climb on foot into the mountains, Kondo said, "Why don't we get married? We'd make a good team. You've got two boys, haven't you? I could adopt them. We're not too old to have more children together. Your family would approve."

Her heart sank at the thought, especially as she knew her family probably would approve.

"You're not married?" It seemed surprising, given his age.

"I was married when I was seventeen, to a Kuroda woman. She died several years ago. We had no children."

Shizuka glanced at him, wondering if he grieved for her.

He said, "She was a very unhappy woman. She was not completely sane. She had long periods when she was tormented by horrible imaginings and fears. She saw ghosts and demons. She was not so bad when I was with her, but I was frequently ordered to travel. I worked as a spy for my mother's family, the Kondo, who had adopted me. On one long trip away I was delayed by bad weather. When I did not return at the expected time, she hanged herself."

For the first time his voice lost its irony. She perceived his real grief and found herself suddenly, unexpectedly moved by him.

"Maybe she was taught too harshly," he said. "I've often wondered what we do to our children. In many ways it was a relief to have none."

"When you're a child, it's like a game," Shizuka said. "I remember being proud of the skills I had, and despising other people for not having them. You don't question the way you're brought up; that's just how it is."

"You are talented; you are the Muto masters' niece and grandchild. Being Kuroda, in the middle, is not so easy. And if you don't have natural talents, the training is very difficult."

He paused and went on quietly: "Possibly she was too sensitive. No upbringing can completely eradicate a person's essential character."

"I wonder. I'm sorry for your loss."

"Well, it was a long time ago. But it certainly made me question a lot of things I'd been taught. Not that I tell most people. When you're part of the Tribe, you're obedient, that's all there is to it."

"Maybe if Takeo had been brought up in the Tribe, he would have learned obedience as we all do," Shizuka said, as if thinking aloud. "He hated being told what to do and he hated being confined. So, what do the Kikuta do? Give him to Akio for training as if he were a two-year-old. They've only themselves to blame for his defection. Shigeru knew how to handle him from the start. He won his loyalty. Takeo would have done anything for him."

As we all would have done, she found herself thinking, and tried to suppress it. She had many secrets concerning Lord Shigeru that only the dead knew, and she was afraid Kondo might discern them.

"What Takeo did was quite considerable," Kondo said, "if you believe all the stories."

"Are you impressed, Kondo? I thought nothing impressed you!"

"Everyone admires courage," he replied. "And, like Takeo, I am also of mixed blood, from both the Tribe and the clans. I was raised by the Tribe until I was twelve and then I became a warrior on the surface, a spy beneath. Maybe I understand something of the conflict he must have gone through."

They walked in silence for a while, then he said, "Anyway, I think you know I am impressed by you."

He was less guarded today, more open in his feeling toward her. She was acutely aware of his desire and, once she had pitied him, less able to resist it. As Arai's mistress or as Kaede's maid, she had had status and the protection status gave her, but now nothing was left to her apart from her own skills and this man who had saved her life and would not make a bad husband. There was no reason not to sleep with him, so after they stopped to eat, around noon, she let him lead her into the shade of the trees. The smell of pine needles and cedar was all around them, the sun warm, the breeze soft. A distant waterfall splashed, muted. Everything spoke of new life and spring. His lovemaking was not as bad as she'd feared, though he was rough and quick compared to Ishida.

Shizuka thought, *If this is what is to be, I must make the best of it.*

And then she thought, *What's happened to me? Have I suddenly got old? A year ago I would have given a man like Kondo short shrift, but a year ago I still thought I was Arai's. And so much has happened since then, so much intrigue, so many deaths: losing Shigeru and Naomi, pretending all the time I did not care; barely able to weep, not even when the father of my children tried to have me murdered, not even when I thought Kaede would die. . . .*

It was not the first time that she had felt sickened by the constant pretense, the ruthlessness, the brutality. She thought of Shigeru and his desire for peace and justice, and of Ishida, who sought to heal, not to kill, and felt her heart twist with more pain than she would have thought possible. *I am old,* she thought. *Next year I will turn thirty.*

Her eyes went hot and she realized she was about to weep. The tears trickled down her face, and Kondo, mistaking them, held her more closely. Her tears lay wet between her cheek and his chest, forming a pool on the vermilion and sepia pictures that were tattooed on his body.

After a while she stood up and went to the waterfall. Dipping a cloth into the icy water, she washed her face, then cupped her hands to drink. The forest around her was silent apart from the croaking of spring frogs and the first tentative cicadas. The air was already cooling. They must hasten if they were to reach the village before nightfall.

Kondo had already picked up their bundles and slung them onto the pole. Now he lifted it to his shoulder.

"You know," he said as they walked on, raising his voice so she could hear him, for she, knowing the path, was in front, "I don't believe you would hurt Takeo. I don't think it would be possible for you to kill him."

"Why not?" she said, turning her head. "I've killed men before!"

"I know your reputation, Shizuka! But when you speak of Takeo, your face softens as if you pity him. And I don't believe you would ever bring grief to Lady Shirakawa because of the strength of your affection for her."

"You see everything! You know everything about me! Are you sure you're not a fox spirit?" She wondered if he had discerned her affair with Ishida and prayed he would not speak of it.

"I have Tribe blood in my veins too," he returned.

"If I am far from Takeo, I will not be torn two ways," she said. "The same goes for you." She walked on for a while in silence and then spoke abruptly. "I suppose I do pity him."

"Yet, people say you are ruthless." His voice had recovered its hint of mockery.

"I can still be moved by suffering. Not the sort people bring on themselves through their own stupidity, but the suffering that is inflicted by fate."

The slope steepened and she felt her breath catch. She did not speak until it lessened again, but she was thinking of the threads that bound her life with Takeo and Kaede, and with the destiny of the Otori.

There was room on the path now for two, and Kondo came up alongside her.

"Takeo's upbringing among the Hidden, his adoption into the warrior class by Shigeru, and the demands of the Tribe seem irreconcilable elements in his life," Shizuka said finally. "They will tear him apart. And now this marriage will arouse more hostility against him."

"I don't suppose he'll live for long. Sooner or later someone will catch up with him."

"You never know," she replied, pretending a lightness she did not feel. "Perhaps it would not be possible for me, or anyone else, to kill him—because we would never get near him."

"Two attempts were made on his way to Terayama," Kondo said. "They both failed and three men died."

"You did not tell me that!"

"I suppose I didn't want to alarm Lady Shirakawa and make her ill again. But with every death the rage against him grows stronger. It's not a way I would like to live."

No, Shizuka thought, *nor would any of us. We would like to live without intrigue and suspicion. We would like to sleep deeply at night, not listening for every unfamiliar sound, fearing the knife through the floor, the poison in the meal, the unseen archer in the forest. At least for a few weeks I can feel safe in the secret village.*

The sun was beginning to set, sending brilliant rays between the cedars and turning their trunks black. The light spilled extravagantly across the forest floor. For the last few minutes Shizuka had been aware that someone was following them.

It must be the children, she thought, and remembered with a flash of clarity how she had honed her own skills as a child in this very area. She knew every rock, every tree, every contour of the land.

"Zenko! Taku!" she called. "Is that you?"

One stifled giggle was the only reply. She thought she

heard footsteps; loose rocks fell somewhere in the distance. The children were taking the quick way home, running up the ridge and down again while she and Kondo followed the winding path. She smiled and tried to shake off her dark mood. She had her sons; she would do whatever seemed best for them. And she would follow her grandparents' advice. Whatever they told her to do, she would do. There was a certain comfort in obedience, and, as Kondo said, it meant everything to the Tribe.

Again, she tried not to think of her own deep disobedience in the past and hoped it would remain buried with the dead.

They left the main path and, clambering over a pile of boulders, followed a smaller one that wound through a craggy ravine. At the far end it made one more twist and began to descend into the valley. Shizuka stopped for a moment; the view never failed to enchant her, the hidden valley in the middle of the rugged mountain country was so surprising. Through the slight haze made up of mist rising from the stream and smoke from hearth fires they could look down on the small collection of buildings, but by the time they had followed the path through the fields the houses stood above them, protected by a strong wooden wall.

The gate, however, was open, and the men guarding it greeted Shizuka cheerfully.

"Hey! Welcome home!"

"Is this how you greet visitors now? Very casual; suppose I was a spy?"

"Your sons already told us you were coming," one of the guards replied. "They saw you on the mountain."

A sweet relief ran through her. She had not realized until this moment the depth of her constant anxiety for them. But they were alive and healthy.

"This is Kondo—" She broke off, realizing she did not know his given name.

"Kondo Kiichi," he said. "My father was Kuroda Tetsuo."

The guards' eyes narrowed as they registered the name, placed him in the Tribe hierarchy, and summed him up by appearance as well as by history. They were cousins or nephews of hers: She had grown up with them, spending months on end with her grandparents, sent there for training while she was still a child. When they were boys she had competed with them, studied and outwitted them. Then her life had led her back to Kumamoto and to Arai.

"Be careful of Shizuka!" one of them now warned Kondo. "I'd sooner sleep with a viper."

"You've got more chance," she retorted.

Kondo said nothing but glanced at her, one eyebrow raised, as they walked on.

From outside, the village buildings looked like ordinary farmhouses, with steep-pitched thatch roofs and faded cedar beams. Farming tools, firewood, sacks of rice, and reed stalks were all stacked away neatly in the sheds at the ends of the buildings. The outer windows were barred with wooden slats and the steps were made from rough-hewn mountain stone. But, within, the houses held many secrets: hidden passageways and entrances, tunnels and cellars, false cupboards and floors, which could conceal the whole community if necessary. Few knew of the existence of this secret village, and even fewer found their way here; yet the Muto family were always ready for attack. And here they trained their children in the ancient traditions of the Tribe.

Shizuka felt an involuntary thrill at the memory of it. Her heartbeat quickened. Nothing since then, not even the fight at Inuyama Castle, came anywhere near the intense excitement of those childhood games.

The main house lay in the center of the village, and at its entrance her family were already waiting to greet her: her grandfather with her two sons and, to her surprise and pleasure, next to the old man, her uncle, Muto Kenji.

"Grandfather, Uncle," she greeted them demurely, and was about to introduce Kondo when the younger boy ran to her excitedly and threw his arms round her waist.

"Taku!" his older brother rebuked him, and then said, "Welcome, Mother. It's been such a long time since we saw you."

"Come here and let me look at you," she said, delighted by their appearance. They had both grown and had lost their childhood chubbiness. Zenko had turned twelve at the beginning of the year, and Taku ten. Even the younger boy had strength and hardness in his muscles, and they both had direct, fearless eyes.

"He is growing like his father," Kenji said, clapping Zenko on the shoulder.

It was true, Shizuka thought, gazing on her older son. He was the image of Arai. Taku, she thought, had more of a Muto look, and he, unlike his brother, bore the straight line of his

Kikuta relatives across his palms. The sharp hearing and other skills might already be manifesting themselves. But she would find out more about that sort of thing later.

Kondo, meanwhile, had knelt before the two Muto masters, telling them his name and parentage.

"He is the one who saved my life," Shizuka said. "You may have heard: There was an attempt to murder me."

"You are not the only one," Kenji said, catching her eye as if to silence her, and indeed, she did not want to say too much in front of the boys. "We'll talk about it later. I'm glad to see you."

A maid came with water to wash the dust from the travelers' feet.

Shizuka's grandfather said to Kondo, "You are very welcome, and we are deeply grateful to you. We met a long time ago; you were only a child, you probably don't remember. Please, come and eat."

As Kondo followed the old man inside, Kenji murmured to Shizuka, "But what has happened? Why are you here? Is Lady Shirakawa all right?"

"Nothing has changed your fondness for her, I see,"

Shizuka replied. "She has joined Takeo in Terayama. I expect they will marry soon—against all my advice, I might add. It is a disaster for them both."

Kenji sighed quietly. She thought she saw a slight smile on his face. "A disaster, probably," he said, "but one ordained by fate."

They stepped inside the house. Taku had run ahead to tell his great-grandmother to bring wine and cups, but Zenko walked quietly next to Kondo.

"Thank you for saving my mother's life, sir," he said formally. "I am in your debt."

"I hope we will get to know each other and be friends," Kondo replied. "Do you like hunting? Maybe you can take me out on the mountain. I've eaten no meat for months."

The boy smiled and nodded. "Sometimes we use traps and, later in the year, falcons. I hope you will still be here then."

He is a man already, Shizuka thought. *If only I could protect him . . . if only they both could stay children forever.*

Her grandmother came with the wine. Shizuka took it from her and served the men. Then she went with the old woman to the kitchen, breathing in deeply, savoring all the familiar smells. The maids, cousins of hers, welcomed her with delight. She wanted to help with the food as she always had, but they would not let her.

"Tomorrow, tomorrow," her grandmother said. "Tonight you can be the honored guest."

Shizuka sat on the edge of the wooden step that led from the earthen-floored kitchen to the main part of the house. She could hear the murmur of the men talking, the higher voices of the boys, Zenko's already breaking.

"Let's drink a cup together," her grandmother said, chuckling. "We didn't expect you, but you're all the more welcome for that. What a jewel, isn't she?" she appealed to the maids, who readily agreed.

"Shizuka is prettier than ever," Kana said. "More like the boys' sister than their mother."

"And she's got a good-looking man in tow as usual." Miyabi laughed. "Did he really save your life? It's like something out of a story."

Shizuka smiled and drank the wine in a gulp, happy for the moment to be home, listening to the sibilant dialect of her relatives as they pressed her for gossip and news.

"They say Lady Shirakawa is the most beautiful woman in the Three Countries," Kana said. "Is it true?"

Shizuka downed another cup, feeling the warmth of the wine hit her stomach and send its cheerful message through her body.

"You've no idea how beautiful," she replied. "You say I'm pretty. Well, men look at me and want to sleep with me, but they look at Shirakawa Kaede and despair. They can't bear the fact that such beauty exists and they will never possess it. I tell you, I was far prouder of her looks than of my own."

"They say she bewitches people," Miyabi said, "and whoever desires her dies."

"She's bewitched your uncle," the old woman cackled. "You should hear him talk about her."

"Why did you leave her?" Kana asked, deftly dropping vegetables sliced as thin as paper into the steamer.

"She's been bewitched herself by love. She's joined Otori Takeo, the Kikuta boy who's caused so much trouble. They are determined to marry. He sent me and Kondo away because the Kikuta have issued an edict against him."

Kana yelped as she steamed her fingers by mistake.

"Ah, what a shame," Miyabi sighed. "They're both doomed, then."

"What do you expect?" Shizuka retorted. "You know the

punishment for disobedience." But the corners of her own eyes grew hot as if she were about to weep.

"Come, come," her grandmother said. She seemed more gentle than Shizuka remembered. "You've had a long journey. You're tired. Eat and get your strength back. Kenji will want to talk to you tonight."

Kana spooned rice from the cooking pot into a bowl and heaped vegetables on top of it. They were the spring vegetables of the mountain, burdock, fern shoots, and wild mushrooms. Shizuka ate where she was, sitting on the step, as she so often had when she was a child.

Miyabi asked delicately, "I have to prepare the beds, but . . . where is the visitor to sleep?"

"He can go with the men," Shizuka replied through a mouthful of rice. "I will be up till late with my uncle."

If they slept together in her family home, it would be as good as announcing their marriage. She was not sure yet; she would do nothing without seeking Kenji's advice.

Her grandmother patted her on the hand, her eyes bright and happy, and poured them both another cup of wine. When the rest of the meal was ready and the girls had taken the trays of food to the men, the old woman got to her feet.

"Take a walk with me. I want to go to the shrine. I'll make an offering in thanks for your safe return."

She took rice balls, wrapped in a cloth, and a small flask of wine. Next to Shizuka she seemed to have shrunk, and she walked more slowly, grateful for her granddaughter's arm to lean on.

Night had fallen. Most people were inside, eating the evening meal or preparing for sleep. A dog barked at the door of one house and bounded toward them but was called back by a woman, who then shouted a greeting to them.

From the thick grove that surrounded the shrine, owls were hooting, and Shizuka's sharp ears caught the high squeaking of bats.

"Can you still hear them?" her grandmother said, peering at the fleeting shapes. "And I can barely see them! That's the Kikuta in you."

"My hearing is nothing special," Shizuka said. "I wish it were."

A stream ran through the grove, and fireflies glowed along the bank. The gates loomed before them, vermilion red in the faint light. They passed beneath them and washed their hands and rinsed their mouths at the fountain. The cistern was of blue-black stone, and a dragon forged from iron kept guard over it. The mountain spring water was icy cold and pure.

Lamps burned in front of the shrine, but it seemed deserted. The old woman placed her offerings on the wooden pedestal in front of the statue of Hachiman, the god of war. She bowed twice, clapped her hands three times, and repeated this ritual three times. Shizuka did the same and found herself praying for the god's protection, not for herself or for her family, but for Kaede and Takeo in the wars that would certainly engulf them. She was almost ashamed of herself and was glad no one could read her thoughts—no one but the god himself.

Her grandmother stood staring upward. Her face seemed as ancient as the carved statue and as full of numinous power. Shizuka felt her strength and her endurance, and was moved by love and reverence for her. She was glad she had come home. The old people had the wisdom of generations; maybe some of that wisdom would be transferred to her.

They remained motionless for a few moments, and then there was a bustle of sound, a door sliding open, footsteps on the veranda. The shrine priest came toward them, already in his evening clothes.

"I didn't expect anyone so late," he said. "Come and drink a cup of tea with us."

"My granddaughter is back."

"Ah, Shizuka! It's been a long time. Welcome home."

They sat with the priest and his wife for a while, chatting casually, catching up with the gossip of the village. Then her grandmother said, "Kenji will be ready for you now. We must not keep him waiting."

They walked back between the darkened houses, now mostly silent. People slept early at this time of year and rose early to start the spring work, preparing the fields and planting. Shizuka recalled the days she had spent as a young woman, ankle-deep in the rice fields, planting the seedlings, sharing her youth and fertility with them, while traditional songs were chanted by the older women on the banks. Was she too old to take part in the spring planting now?

If she married Kondo, would she be too old to have another child?

The girls were cleaning up the kitchen and scouring the

dishes when they returned. Taku was sitting where Shizuka had sat earlier, his eyes closing, his head nodding.

"He has a message for you." Miyabi laughed. "Wouldn't give it to anyone but you!"

Shizuka sat down beside him and tickled his cheek. "Messengers can't fall asleep," she teased.

"Uncle Kenji is ready to talk to you now," Taku said importantly, and then spoiled the effect by yawning. "He's in the living room with Grandfather, and everyone else has gone to bed."

"Where you should be," Shizuka said, pulling him into her arms. She hugged him tightly and he relaxed against her like a little boy, nuzzling his head into her breasts. After a few moments he began to wriggle and said in a muffled voice, "Don't keep Uncle Kenji waiting, Mother."

She laughed and released him. "Go to bed."

"Will you still be here in the morning?" He yawned again.

"Of course!"

He gave her a sweet smile. "I'll show you everything I've learned since I last saw you."

"Your mother will be astonished," Miyabi said.

Shizuka walked with her younger son to the women's

room, where he still slept. Tonight she would have him next to her, hear his childish breathing through the night, and wake in the morning to see the relaxed limbs and the tousled hair. She had missed that so much.

Zenko slept in the men's room now; she could hear his voice questioning Kondo about the battle of Kushimoto, where he had fought with Arai. She heard the note of pride in the boy's voice when he mentioned his father's name. How much did he know of Arai's campaign against the Tribe, of his attempt on her life?

What will happen to them? she thought. *Will their mixed blood be as destructive to them as Takeo's?*

She said good night to Taku, walked through the room, and slid the door open to the next room, where her uncle and grandfather sat waiting for her. She knelt before them, touching her brow to the matting. Kenji smiled and nodded, saying nothing. He looked at his father and raised his eyebrows.

"Well, well," the old man said. "I must leave you two together."

As Shizuka helped him to his feet, she was struck by how much he, too, had aged. She walked with him to the door, where Kana was waiting to help him get ready for bed.

"Good night, child," he said. "What a relief it is to have you here in safety in these dark days. But how long will we be safe anywhere?"

"Surely he's being overly pessimistic," she said to her uncle as she returned. "Arai's rage will subside. He'll realize he cannot eradicate the Tribe and that he needs spies like any other warlord. He'll come to terms with us."

"I agree. No one sees Arai as a problem in the long term. It would be easy enough to lie low until he's calmed down, as you say. But there is another matter that could be far more serious. It seems Shigeru left us an unexpected legacy. The Kikuta believe he kept records of our networks and members and that these records are now in Takeo's possession."

Her heart stopped in her throat. It seemed to her that she had brought the past to life just by thinking about it.

"Is it possible?" she replied, trying to respond normally.

"The Kikuta master Kotaro is convinced of it. At the end of last year he sent Takeo to Hagi, with Akio, to locate the records and bring them back. It seems Takeo went to Shigeru's house, saw Ichiro, and then got away from Akio somehow and headed for Terayama. He evaded and killed two agents and an Otori warrior on the way."

"An Otori warrior?" Shizuka repeated stupidly.

"Yes, the Kikuta are stepping up their contacts with the Otori, both in alliance against Arai and to eliminate Takeo."

"And the Muto?"

Kenji grunted. "I have not made a decision yet."

Shizuka raised her eyebrows and waited for him to go on.

"Kotaro is assuming the records were being looked after at the temple, which in hindsight seems obvious to me. That wicked old Matsuda never gave up plotting despite becoming a priest, and he and Shigeru were very close. I think I can even recall the chest Shigeru carried them in. I can't imagine how I overlooked it. My only excuse is that I had other things on my mind at that time. The Kikuta are furious with me, and I'm left looking like an idiot." He grinned ruefully. "Shigeru outfoxed me—me, whom they used to call the Fox!"

"That explains the edict against Takeo," Shizuka said. "I thought it was for disobedience. It seemed fierce, but it didn't surprise me. When I heard he was working with Akio, I knew there would be trouble."

"My daughter said so too. She sent a message to me while Takeo was still in our house in Yamagata. There was some incident: He outwitted my wife and escaped for a night, nothing major, and he came back by morning, but Yuki wrote then that he and Akio would end up killing each other. Akio very nearly did die, by the way. Muto Yuzuru's men pulled him out of the river, half-drowned and half-frozen."

"Takeo should have finished him off," Shizuka couldn't help saying.

Kenji smiled without mirth. "I'm afraid that was my first reaction too. Akio claimed he tried to prevent Takeo from getting away, but I learned later from Yuki that he was already under instructions to kill him, once the whereabouts of the records had been discovered."

"Why?" Shizuka said. "What good does his death do to them?"

"It's not a simple situation. Takeo's appearance has disturbed a lot of people, especially among the Kikuta. His lack of obedience and his recklessness don't help."

"The Kikuta sound so extreme, whereas you always seemed to give Takeo a lot of leeway," Shizuka said.

"It was the only way to handle him. I learned that as soon as I got to Hagi. He's got good instincts, he'll do anything for you if you win his loyalty, but you can't force him. He'll break rather than give in."

"Must be a Kikuta trait," Shizuka murmured.

"Maybe." Kenji sighed deeply and stared into the shadows. He did not speak for a while, then said, "For the Kikuta, everything is black-and-white: You obey or you die . . . the only cure for stupidity is death . . . all the things they're brought up to believe."

If the Kikuta ever find out my part in all this, they will kill me, Shizuka thought. *I dare not tell Kenji either.* "So now Takeo is not only lost to the Tribe, but holds information with which he can destroy us?"

"Yes, and that information will buy him an alliance with Arai sooner or later."

"He will never be allowed to live," Shizuka said with renewed sorrow.

"He's survived so far. It's proved harder than the Kikuta thought it would be to get rid of him." Shizuka thought she detected a note of rueful pride in her uncle's voice. "And he has the knack of surrounding himself with devoted followers. Half the Otori clan's young warriors have already crossed the border to join him in Terayama."

"If he and Kaede marry, as I am sure they will," Shizuka said, "Arai will be enraged. It may take more than Shigeru's records to placate him."

"Well, you know Arai better than anyone. There's also the question of his sons, and of you. I haven't told the boys that their father ordered your death, but they're sure to find out sooner or later. It won't bother Taku—he's Tribe through and through—but Zenko idolizes his father. He's not going to be as talented as Taku, and in many ways it would be better for him to be raised by Arai. Is there any possibility of it?"

"I don't know," Shizuka said. "The more land he conquers, the more sons he will want, I would imagine."

"We should send someone to him to see how he's reacting—to Takeo's marriage, to the Otori—and how he feels toward the boys. What about Kondo? Shall I send him?"

"Why not?" Shizuka replied with a certain relief.

"Kondo seems fond of you. Will you marry him?"

"He wants it," she said. "I told him I had to ask your advice. But I would like more time to think about it."

"No need to rush into anything," Kenji agreed. "You can give him your answer when he returns." His eyes gleamed with some emotion that she could not read. "And I can decide what action to take."

Shizuka said nothing, but she studied Kenji's face in the lamplight, trying to make sense of all the pieces of information he had given her, trying to decipher the unspoken as much as the spoken. She felt he was glad to be able to share these concerns with her and guessed he had not told anyone else, not even his own parents. She was aware of the great affection he had had for Shigeru and still held for Takeo, and could imagine the conflict that having to collaborate in Takeo's death would cause him. She had never known him, or any other Tribe member, to speak so openly of divisions between the masters.

If the Muto and the Kikuta families were to fall out, could the Tribe survive? It seemed an even greater danger to her than anything Arai or Takeo might do.

"Where is your daughter now?" she asked.

"As far as I know, she is in one of the secret Kikuta villages north of Matsue." Kenji paused and then said quietly, almost painfully, "Yuki was married to Akio at the beginning of the year."

"*To Akio?*" Shizuka could not help exclaiming.

"Yes, poor girl. The Kikuta insisted and there was no way I could refuse them. There had been talk of a match between them ever since they were both children. I had no rational grounds for withholding my consent anyway, just the irrational sentiments of the father of an only child. My wife did not share these. She was strongly in favor, especially as Yuki was already pregnant."

Shizuka was astonished. "With Akio's child?"

He shook his head. She had never before seen her uncle unable to speak like this.

"Not Takeo's?"

He nodded. The lamps flickered; the house lay silent.

Shizuka could think of nothing to say in response. All she could think of was the child Kaede had lost. She seemed to hear the question again that Kaede had asked her in the garden at Shirakawa: *Would they have taken the child as they took Takeo?* That the Tribe should have a child of Takeo's seemed like something supernatural to her, the cruel workings of fate that humans cannot hope to escape, turn and twist as they might.

Kenji took a deep breath and went on: "She became infatuated with Takeo after the incident at Yamagata, and took his side strongly against the Kikuta master and me. As you might imagine, I myself was in considerable anguish over the decision to take Takeo in Inuyama before the assassination attempt on Iida. I betrayed Shigeru. I don't think I will ever forgive myself for the part I played in his death. For years I considered him my closest friend. However, for the sake of unity within the Tribe, I did as the Kikuta desired and delivered Takeo to them. But between you and me, I would have been happy to have died at Inuyama if that could have erased the shame I felt. I have not spoken of this to anyone except you.

"Of course, the Kikuta are delighted to have the child. It will be born in the seventh month. They hope it will inherit the skills of both its parents. They blame Takeo's upbringing for all his defects; they intend to raise this child themselves from birth—"

He broke off. The silence in the room deepened. "Say something, Niece, even if it's only that it serves me right!"

"It is not for me to judge you for anything you have done," she replied in a low voice. "I am sorry for all you must have suffered. I am amazed at the way fate plays with us like pieces on a board."

"Do you ever see ghosts?"

"I dream of Lord Shirakawa," she admitted. After a long pause she added, "You know that Kondo and I brought about his death to preserve Kaede and her child."

She heard the hiss of his breath, but he did not speak, and after a few moments she continued. "Her father was out of his mind, on the point of violating and then killing her. I wanted to save her life and the child's. But she lost it anyway and nearly died. I don't know if she remembers what we did, and I would not hesitate to do the same thing again; but for some reason, perhaps because I have never spoken of it to anyone, not even Kondo, it haunts me."

"If it was to save her life, I'm sure your action was justified," he replied.

"It was one of those moments when there was no time to think. Kondo and I acted instinctively. I had never killed a man of such high rank before. It seems like a crime to me."

"Well, my betrayal of Shigeru also seems like a crime. He visits me in dreams. I see him as he looked when we brought him up out of the river. I drew the hood from his face and asked him to forgive me, but he only had strength to speak to Takeo. Night after night he comes to me." There was another long silence.

"What are you thinking of?" she whispered. "You would not split the Tribe?"

"I must do what seems best for the Muto family," he replied. "And the Kikuta have my daughter and will soon have my grandchild. Obviously these are my first obligations. But I swore to Takeo when I first met him that while I was alive he would be safe. I will not seek his death. We'll wait and see which way he jumps. The Kikuta want the Otori to provoke him and lure him into battle. They've been concentrating all their attention on Hagi and Terayama." He hissed through his teeth. "I suppose poor old Ichiro will be their first target. But what do you think Takeo and Kaede will do once they're married?"

"Kaede is determined to inherit Maruyama," Shizuka replied. "I imagine they will move south as soon as possible."

"Maruyama has only a few Tribe families," Kenji said. "Takeo will be safer there than anywhere." He was silent, wrapped in his thoughts. Then he smiled slightly. "Of course, we can only blame ourselves for the marriage. We brought them together; we encouraged them, even. Whatever can have possessed us?"

Shizuka recalled suddenly the training hall in Tsuwano,

heard the clash of the wooden poles, the rain pouring down outside, saw their faces young and vivid, on the threshold of passion. "Perhaps we felt sorry for them. They were both pawns being used in a conspiracy wider than either of them suspected, both likely to die before they had begun to live."

"Or perhaps you are right and we were the pawns, moved by the hand of fate," her uncle replied. "Kondo can leave tomorrow. Stay here for the summer. It will be good to talk about these things with you. I have deep decisions to make that will affect many generations to come."

· 5 ·

The first weeks in Maruyama were spent as Kaede had predicted, in restoring the land. Our welcome was warm and seemingly wholehearted, but Maruyama was an extensive domain with many hereditary retainers and a large body of elders who were as opinionated and conservative as most old men. My reputation as Shigeru's avenger stood me in good stead, but the usual rumors surfaced about how I had achieved it: my doubtful origins, the hint of sorcery. My own Otori warriors were completely loyal and I trusted Sugita, his family, and the men who had fought alongside him, but I had my suspicions of many of the others, and they were equally suspicious of me.

Sugita was delighted by our marriage and confided in me what he had once said to Kaede that he believed I might unite the Three Countries and bring peace. But the elders generally were surprised by it. No one dared say anything to my face, but from hints and whispered conversations I soon gathered that a marriage to Fujiwara had been expected. It did not bother me particularly—I had no idea then of the extent of the nobleman's power and influence—but like everything else that summer it added to my sense of urgency. I had to move against Hagi; I had to take over the leadership of the Otori clan. Once I had gained what was legally mine and had my base in Hagi, no one would dare question or challenge me.

In the meantime my wife and I became farmers, riding out every day with Sugita, inspecting fields, woods, villages, and rivers, ordering repairs, clearing away dead trees, pruning, and planting. The land was well surveyed and the taxation system sound and not unjust. The domain was rich, although neglected, and its people hardworking and enterprising. They needed very little encouragement to return to the level of activity and prosperity they had enjoyed under Lady Naomi.

The castle and residence were also somewhat neglected, but as Kaede set about restoring them they quickly regained the beauty created by Naomi. The matting was replaced, screens repainted, wooden floors polished. In the garden stood the tea room built by Naomi's grandmother that she had told me about the first time I had met her in Chigawa. She had promised me that one day we would drink tea there together, and when the redecoration of the simple rustic building was completed and Kaede prepared tea there, I felt that the promise had been fulfilled, even though Naomi herself was no longer alive.

I was conscious of Naomi's spirit, and Shigeru's, with us at all times. As the abbot had said in Terayama, in Kaede and me they seemed to have the chance to live again. We would achieve everything they had dreamed of but had been thwarted in. We placed tablets and offerings in a small shrine deep within the residence, and prayed before it every day for guidance and help. I had a profound sense of relief that I was finally carrying out Shigeru's last requests to me, and Kaede seemed happier than she had ever been before.

It would have been a time of great joy, celebrating victory and seeing the land and the people begin to flourish again, had it not been for the darker work I felt compelled to undertake, a work that gave me no pleasure at all. Sugita tried to

tell me there were no Tribe members in the castle town, so
well hidden were they and so secret their operations. But I
knew better, for Shigeru had chronicled them all, and I had
not forgotten the men Hiroshi had described, who had
appeared out of the air, clad in dark clothes, and killed his
father. We had found no such bodies among the dead at
Asagawa. They had survived the battle and would now be
stalking me.

Of the families listed in the records, most were Kuroda
and Imai, a few of the richer merchants Muto. There were
very few Kikuta this far to the west, but the one existing
family maintained their customary authority over the
others. I clung to the words of the prophecy that had told
me that only my own son could kill me, but even though by
day I might believe it I still was alert to every sound, slept
lightly at night, ate only food that Manami had prepared or
supervised.

I had heard nothing of Yuki and did not know if her
child was born or if it was a boy. Kaede continued to bleed
regularly throughout the summer, and though I knew she was
disappointed not to conceive a child, I could not help feeling
a certain relief. I longed for children of our own, but I feared

the complications they would bring. And what would I do if Kaede bore me a son?

How to deal with the Tribe was a problem that constantly exercised my mind. The first week I was in the town I sent messages to the Kikuta and Muto families informing them that I wished to consult with them and they were to wait on me the following day. That night there was an attempt to break into the residence and steal the records. I woke to hear someone in the room, perceived his barely visible form, challenged him, and pursued him to the outer gates, hoping to take him alive. He lost invisibility as he leaped over the wall and was killed by the guards on the other side before I could prevent it. He was dressed in black and tattooed like Shintaro, the assassin who had tried to kill Shigeru in Hagi. I placed him as one of the Kuroda family.

I sent men the next morning to the Kikuta house and had everyone in it arrested. Then I waited to see who would keep the appointment with me. Two old Muto men turned up, wily and slippery. I gave them the option of leaving the province or renouncing their Tribe loyalties. They said they would have to speak with their children. Nothing happened for two days; then a hidden bowman tried to shoot me as I rode with Amano and Sugita in a remote country area. Shun and I heard the sound together and evaded the arrow; we hunted down the bowman, hoping to get information from him, but he took poison. I thought he might have been the second man Hiroshi had seen, but I had no way of knowing for sure.

By this time I had run out of patience. I thought the Tribe were playing with me, suspecting I would never have the ruthlessness to deal with them. I had all the adults in the Kikuta family I had taken hanged and that night sent patrols to fifty or more houses, with orders to kill everyone in them except children. I hoped to spare the lives of the young ones, but the Tribe poisoned their own children rather than give them to me. The old men came back to me, but my offer had expired. The only choice they were given now was between poison or the sword. They both took poison on the spot.

A few fled from the province. I did not have the resources to track them down. Most sat tight, concealed in secret rooms as I had once been or in hidden villages in the mountains. No one would have been able to ferret them out except me, who knew everything about them and had been trained by them in their own ways. I was privately sickened by my own ruthlessness and horrified that I was massacring families just as my own had been massacred, but I saw no alternative and I do not think I was cruel. I gave them swift deaths; I did not crucify them or burn them alive or hang them upside down by the heels. My aim was to eradicate an evil, not to terrorize the people.

It was not a popular measure with the warrior class, who had benefited from the services of these merchants, had been supplied with soy products and wine, had borrowed money, and occasionally taken advantage of the other, darker trade of murder. It added to their mistrust of me. I tried to keep them busy training men and maintaining the borders while I supervised the recovery of the economy. I'd dealt the merchant class a terrible blow by removing its Tribe component, but on the other hand I'd taken all their assets for the domain itself and had set a great deal of wealth, previously tied up by them, circulating through the system. For two weeks it seemed we would be faced with a shortage of essential goods before winter, but then we uncovered a group of enterprising peasants who, fed up with the extortion of the Tribe, had been distilling and fermenting on a small scale in secret and who knew enough about the process to take over production.

We provided the money to set them up in the Tribe's former premises, and in return took sixty parts out of a hundred for the domain treasury. This promised to be so lucrative a practice it seemed we would need to take no more than thirty parts from the rice harvest, which in turn made us popular with the farmers and villagers.

I distributed the Tribe's other lands and assets to those who had come with me from Terayama. One small hamlet on the banks of a river was given over to the outcasts, who immediately set about tanning the skins taken from the dead horses. I was relieved that this group who had helped me so much was now settled peacefully, but my protection of them baffled the elders and increased their suspicions.

Every week a few more Otori warriors turned up to join me. The main Otori army that had tried to surround me at Terayama had pursued me as far as the river we had crossed on the outcasts' bridge, and was still camped there, controlling the roads between Yamagata, Inuyama, and the West and, apparently, giving Arai a few anxieties too.

I joined Kaede most afternoons in the tea room, where, together with Makoto and the Miyoshi brothers, we discussed strategy. My main fear was that if I stayed where I was for too long, I would be encircled by the Otori to the North and Arai to the Southeast. I knew Arai was likely to return to his own town, Kumamoto, during the summer. I could not hope to fight on two fronts. We decided that now was a good time to send Kahei and Gemba to Arai to try to make peace of some kind for however short a period. I was aware I had very little to bargain with: our brief alliance against Iida, Shigeru's legacy, and the records of the Tribe. On the other hand, I had enraged him by my earlier disappearance and insulted him by my marriage, and for all I knew, his anger against the Tribe might already have been tempered by expediency.

I had no illusions about peace with the Otori. I could not negotiate with Shigeru's uncles and they would never abdicate in my favor. The clan was already so divided that it was for all intents in a state of civil war. If I attacked their main force, even if we were victorious, they would simply fall back to Hagi, where they could easily hold us off until winter itself defeated us. Despite the recovery of the Maruyama domain, we did not have the resources for a long siege at such a distance from our home base.

I'd escaped from the Otori army by using the outcasts, whom no one else had dreamed of approaching, and now I began to wonder how I might take them by surprise again. When I thought of the city, I saw it lying in the cup of the bay, so defensible on its landward side, so open to the sea. If I could not get to Hagi by land, might I not be able to go by water?

Troops that could be transported rapidly by sea: I knew of no warlord who had such a force. Yet history tells us that hundreds of years ago a huge army sailed from the mainland and would have been victorious had the Eight Islands not been saved by a storm sent from heaven. My thoughts kept turning to the boy who'd been my friend in Hagi, Terada Fumio, who had fled with his family to the island of Oshima. Fumio had taught me about ships and sailing, he had taught me to swim, and he had hated Shigeru's uncles as much as I did. Could I turn him into an ally now?

I did not speak openly of these ideas, but one night, after the others had retired, Kaede—who watched me all the time and knew all my moods—said, "You are thinking of attacking Hagi in some other way?"

"When I lived there I became friendly with the son of a family, the Terada, who had been fishermen. The Otori lords raised the taxation of their catch to such an extent that they took their boats and moved to Oshima; it's an island off the northwest coast."

"They became pirates?"

"Their markets were closed to them; it was impossible to live by fishing alone. I'm thinking of paying them a visit. If the Terada have enough resources and they are willing to help me, it would be possible to take Hagi by sea. But it must be done this year, and that means I must go before the typhoons begin."

"Why do you have to go yourself?" Kaede asked. "Send a messenger."

"Fumio will trust me, but I don't think his family will talk to anyone else. Now that the rains are over, Kahei and Gemba must go at once to Inuyama. I'll go with a few men, Makoto, Jiro, maybe."

"Let me come with you," Kaede said.

I thought of the complexities of traveling with my wife, of bringing one woman at least to accompany her, of finding suitable accommodation.

"No, stay here with Sugita. I don't want us both to be absent from the domain at the same time. Amano must stay here too."

"I wish I were Makoto," she said. "I am jealous of him."

"He is jealous of you," I said lightly. "He thinks I spend far too much time talking to you. A wife is for one thing, providing heirs. Everything else a man should look for in his comrades."

I had been joking, but she took me seriously. "I should give you a child." Her lips were pressed together and I saw her eyes moisten with tears. "Sometimes I am afraid I will never conceive again. I wish our child had not died."

"We will have other children," I said. "All girls, all as beautiful as their mother." I took her in my arms. It was a warm, still night, but her skin felt cold and she was shivering.

"Don't go," she said.

"I will only be away a week at most."

The next day the Miyoshi brothers set out for Inuyama to plead my cause with Arai, and I left with Makoto for the coast the day after. Kaede was still upset and we parted with a slight coolness between us. It was our first disagreement. She wanted to come with me; I could have let her, but I did not. I did not know how long it would be or how much we would both suffer before I saw her again.

Still, I rode out cheerfully enough with Makoto, Jiro, and

three men. We went in unmarked traveling clothes so we could move swiftly and without formalities. I was happy to be leaving the castle town for a while and happy, too, to be able to set aside the ruthless work I'd undertaken to eradicate the Tribe. The plum rains had ended, the air was clear, the sky deep blue. Along the road we saw signs everywhere of the land's gradual return to prosperity. The rice fields were brilliant green, the harvest would be brought in; this winter, at least, no one would starve.

Makoto was silent and reserved in Kaede's presence, but when we were alone together we talked as only the closest friends can. He had seen me at my weakest and my most vulnerable, and I trusted him as I trusted no one else. I opened my heart to him, and, apart from Kaede, only he knew of my constant expectation of attack from the Tribe and my deep dislike of what I had to do to eradicate them. The only thing that pained him about me was the depth of my love for Kaede. He was jealous, perhaps, though he tried to hide it; but, over and above that, he thought there was something unnatural about it: It was not seemly for a man to feel such passion for his wife. He did not speak of it, but I read the disapproval in his expression.

He had taken Jiro under his wing with his usual unobtrusive thoughtfulness and found the time to teach him writing as well as training with the pole and spear. Jiro proved quick to learn. He seemed to grow several inches over the summer and began to fill out, too, now that he was eating properly. Occasionally, I suggested that he return to his family in Kibi and help with the harvest there, but he begged to be allowed to stay, swearing he would serve either me or Makoto for the rest of his life. He was typical of most of the farmers' sons who had come to fight for me: quick-witted, courageous, strong. We armed them with long spears and fitted them out with leather armor, dividing them into units of twenty men, each with its own leader. Any who showed the right aptitude we trained as bowmen. I counted them among my greatest assets.

On the afternoon of the third day we came to the coast. It was not as bleak as around Matsue; indeed, on that late-summer day, it looked beautiful. Several steep-sided islands rose abruptly from a tranquil sea whose color was deep blue, almost indigo. The breeze ruffled the surface into triangular waves like knife blades. The islands seemed uninhabited, with nothing breaking the solid green of the pines and cedars that clung to them.

Far in the distance, just visible in the haze, we could make out the bulky shape of Oshima, the cone of its volcano hidden in the clouds. Beyond it, out of sight, lay the city of Hagi.

"Presumably that's the dragon's lair," Makoto said. "And how do you intend to approach it?"

From the cliff where our horses stood, the road led down to a small bay where there was a fishing village—a few hovels, boats pulled up on the shingle, the gates of a shrine to the sea god.

"We could take a boat from there," I said doubtfully, for the place looked deserted. The fires that the fishermen burn to get salt from seawater were no more than piles of black and charred logs, and there was no sign of movement.

"I've never been in a boat," Jiro exclaimed, "except across the river!"

"Nor have I," Makoto muttered to me as we turned the horses' heads toward the village.

The villagers had already seen us and gone into hiding. As we approached the hovels they tried to run away. The beauty of the place was deceptive; I'd seen many impoverished people throughout the Three Countries, but these were far and away the poorest and the most wretched. My men ran after one of them who was stumbling across the shingle, carrying a child of about two years. They caught up with him easily, hampered as he was by his son, and dragged them both back. The child was wailing, but the father had the look of a man beyond grief or fear.

"We are not going to hurt you or take anything from you," I said. "I'm looking for someone to go with me to Oshima."

He glanced up at me, disbelief written in his face. One of the men holding him cuffed him hard.

"Speak when His Lordship questions you!"

"His Lordship? Being a lord won't save him from Terada. You know what we call Oshima? The entrance to hell."

"Hell or not, I have to go there," I replied. "And I'll pay for it."

"What good is silver to us?" he said, bitterly. "If anyone knows I have silver, they'll kill me for it. I'm only alive because I have nothing left worth stealing. Bandits have already taken my wife and my daughters. My son was not weaned when they kidnapped his mother. I nursed him on rags dipped in water and brine. I chewed fish and fed him from my own mouth like a seabird. I cannot leave him to go with you to certain death at Oshima."

"Then find us someone who will take me," I said. "When we return to Maruyama we'll send soldiers to destroy the bandits. The domain now belongs to my wife, Shirakawa Kaede. We will make this place safe for you."

"Doesn't matter who it belongs to, Your Lordship will never return from Oshima."

"Take the child," Makoto ordered the men angrily, saying to the fisherman, "He will die unless you obey!"

"Take him!" the man shrieked. "Kill him! I should have done so myself. Then kill me and my suffering will be over!"

Makoto leaped from his horse to seize the child himself. It clung to its father's neck like a monkey, sobbing noisily.

"Leave them," I said, dismounting, too, and giving the reins to Jiro. "We cannot force them." I studied the man, taking care not to meet his gaze; after his first quick glance he did not look at me again. "What food do we have?"

Jiro opened the saddlebags and brought out rice wrapped in kelp and flavored with pickled plums, and dried fish.

"I want to talk to you alone," I said to the man. "Will you and the child sit down and eat with me?"

He swallowed hard, his gaze fixed on the food. The child

smelled the fish and turned its head. It held out one hand toward Jiro.

The father nodded.

"Let him go," I said to the men, and took the food from Jiro. Outside one of the hovels was an upturned boat. "We'll sit there."

I walked toward it and the man followed. I sat and he knelt at my feet, bowing his head. He placed the child on the sand and pushed its head down too. It had stopped sobbing but sniffed loudly from time to time.

I held out the food and whispered the first prayer of the Hidden over it, watching the man's face all the time.

His mouth formed words. He did not take the food. The child reached out for it, beginning to wail again. The father said, "If you are trying to trap me, may the Secret One forgive you." He said the second prayer and took the rice ball. Breaking it into pieces, he fed it to his son. "At least my child will have tasted rice before he dies."

"I am not trying to trap you." I handed him another rice ball, which he crammed into his mouth. "I am Otori Takeo, heir to the Otori clan. But I was raised among the Hidden and my childhood name was Tomasu."

"May he bless and keep you," he said, taking the fish from me. "How did you pick me?"

"When you said you should have killed yourself and your son, your eyes flickered upward as if you were praying."

"I have prayed many times for the Secret One to take me to him. But you know it is forbidden for me to kill myself or my son."

"Are you all Hidden here?"

"Yes, for generations, since the first teachers came from the mainland. We've never been persecuted for it as such. The lady of the domain who died last year used to protect us. But bandits and pirates grow bolder and more numerous all the time, and they know we cannot fight back."

He broke off a piece of fish and gave it to the child. Holding it in his fist, the boy stared at me. His eyes were red-rimmed and sticky, his face filthy and streaked with tears. He suddenly gave me a small, wavering smile.

"As I told you, my wife inherited this domain from Lady Maruyama. I swear to you we will clear it of all bandits and make it safe for you. I knew Terada's son in Hagi and I need to speak to him."

"There's one man who may help you. He has no children,

and I've heard he's been to Oshima. I'll try to find him. Go to the shrine. The priests ran away, so there's no one there, but you can use the buildings and leave your horses and men there. If he's willing to take you, he'll come to you tonight. It's half a day's sailing to Oshima, and you'll need to leave on the high tide—morning or evening, I'll leave that to him."

"You won't regret helping us," I said.

For the first time a smile flickered across his face. "Your Lordship may regret it once you get to Oshima."

I stood and began to walk away. I'd gone no more than ten paces when he called to me, "Sir! Lord Otori!"

When I turned he ran to me, the child toddling after him, still sucking on the fish. He said awkwardly, "You will kill, then?"

"Yes," I said, "I have killed and I will kill again, even if I am damned for it."

"May He have mercy on you," he whispered.

The sun was setting in a blaze of vermilion, and long shadows lay across the black shingle. Seabirds called in harsh mournful voices like lost souls. The waves sucked and dragged at the stones with a heavy sighing.

The shrine buildings were decaying, the timbers coated

in lichen, rotting away beneath the moss-covered trees, which had been twisted into grotesque shapes by the north winds of winter. Now, though, the night was windless, oppressive, and still, the sighing of the waves echoed by the shrill of cicadas and the whine of mosquitoes. We let the horses graze in the unkempt garden and drink from the ponds. These were empty of fish, which had all been eaten long since; a solitary frog croaked forlornly and occasionally owls hooted.

Jiro made a fire, burning green wood to keep the insects away, and we ate a little of the food we'd brought with us, rationing ourselves since we obviously would not find anything to eat here. I told the men to sleep first; we would wake them at midnight. I could hear their voices whispering for a while and then their breathing became even.

"If this man doesn't show up tonight, what then?" Makoto asked.

"I believe he will come," I replied.

Jiro was silent by the fire, his head rolling forward as he fought sleep.

"Lie down," Makoto told him, and when the boy had fallen into the sudden slumber of his age, he said quietly to me, "What did you say to tame the fisherman?"

"I fed his child," I replied. "Sometimes that's enough."

"It was more than that. He was listening to you as though you spoke the same language."

I shrugged. "We'll see if this other fellow turns up."

Makoto said, "It is the same with the outcast. He dares approach you as if he has some claim on you, and speaks to you almost as an equal. I wanted to kill him for his insolence at the river, but you listened to him and he to you."

"Jo-An saved my life on the road to Terayama."

"You even know his name," Makoto said. "I have never known an outcast by name in my entire life."

My eyes were stinging from the smoky fire. I did not reply. I had never told Makoto that I'd been born into the Hidden and raised by them. I had told Kaede but no one else. It was something I'd been brought up never to speak of and maybe the only teaching I still obeyed.

"You've talked about your father," Makoto said. "I know he was of mixed Tribe and Otori blood. But you never mention your mother. Who was she?"

"She was a peasant woman from Mino. It's a tiny village in the mountains on the other side of Inuyama, almost on the borders of the Three Countries. No one's ever heard of it. Perhaps that's why I have a strong bond with outcasts and fishermen."

I tried to speak lightly. I did not want to think about my mother. I had traveled so far from my life with her, and from the beliefs I had been raised in, that when I did think of her it made me uneasy. Not only had I survived when all my people had died, but I no longer believed in what they had died for. I had other goals now—other, far more pressing concerns.

"Was? She's no longer alive?"

In the silent, neglected garden, the fire smoking, the sea sighing, a tension grew between us. He wanted to know my deepest secrets; I wanted to open my heart to him. Now that everyone else slept and only we were awake in this eerie place, maybe desire also crept in. I was always aware of his love for me; it was something I had come to count on, like the loyalty of the Miyoshi brothers, like my love for Kaede. Makoto was a constant in my world. I needed him. Our relationship might have changed since the night he had comforted me at Terayama, but at this moment I remembered how lonely and vulnerable I had been after Shigeru's death, how I had felt I could tell him anything.

The fire had died down so I could barely see his face, but I was aware of his eyes on me. I wondered what he suspected; it seemed so obvious to me that I thought at any moment he would come out with it himself.

I said, "My mother was one of the Hidden. I was brought up in their beliefs. She and all my family, as far as I know, were massacred by the Tohan. Shigeru rescued me. Jo-An and this fisherman are also from the Hidden. We . . . recognize each other."

He said nothing. I went on: "I'm trusting you to tell no one."

"Did our abbot know?"

"He never mentioned it to me, but Shigeru may have told him. Anyway, I am no longer a believer. I've broken all the commandments, particularly the commandment not to kill."

"Of course I will never repeat it. It would do you irreparable harm among the warrior class. Most of them thought Iida was justified in his persecution of them, and not a few emulated him. It explains many things about you that I did not understand."

"You, as a warrior and a monk, a follower of the Enlightened One, must hate the Hidden."

"Not hate so much as feel baffled by their mysterious beliefs. I know so little about them, and what I do know is probably distorted. Maybe one day we'll discuss it when we are at peace."

I heard in his voice an effort to be rational, not to hurt me. "The main thing I learned from my mother was compassion," I said. "Compassion and an aversion to cruelty. But my teaching since then has all been to eradicate compassion and reinforce ruthlessness."

"These are the requirements of government and war," he replied. "That is the path fate leads us along. At the temple we are also taught not to kill, but only saints at the end of their active life can aspire to that. To fight to defend yourself, to avenge your lord, or to bring justice and peace is no sin."

"So Shigeru taught me."

There was a moment of silence when I thought he would reach out to me. To be honest, I would not have recoiled. I felt a sudden longing to lie down and be held by someone. I might even have made the slightest of movements toward him. But he was the one who withdrew. Rising to his feet, he said, "Get some sleep. I'll watch for a while and wake the men shortly."

I stayed close to the fire to keep the mosquitoes away, but

they still whined around my head. The sea continued its ceaseless surge and ebb on the shingle. I was uneasy about what I had revealed, about my own faithlessness, and about what Makoto would now think of me. Childishly, I would have liked him to reassure me that it made no difference. I wanted Kaede. I feared I would disappear into the dragon's lair at Oshima and never see her again.

Sleep finally came. For the first time since my mother's death I dreamed vividly of her. She stood in front of me, outside our house in Mino. I could smell food cooking and heard the chink of the ax as my stepfather cut firewood. In the dream I felt a rush of joy and relief that they were after all still alive. But there was a scrabbling noise at my feet and I could feel something crawling over me. My mother looked down with empty, surprised eyes. I wanted to see what she was looking at and followed her gaze. The ground was a black, heaving mass of crabs, their shells ripped from their backs. Then the screaming began, the sound I'd heard from another shrine, a lifetime away, as a man was torn apart by the Tohan.

I knew the crabs were going to tear me apart as I had torn the shells from them.

I woke up in horror, sweating. Makoto was kneeling beside me. "A man has come," he said. "He will speak only to you."

The feeling of dread was heavy on me. I did not want to go with this stranger to Oshima. I wanted to return at once to Maruyama, to Kaede. I wished I could send someone else on what was most likely a fool's errand. But anyone else would probably be killed by the pirates before any message could be delivered. Having come this far, having been sent this man who would take me to Oshima and the Terada, I could not turn back.

The man was kneeling behind Makoto. I was unable to see much of him in the dark. He apologized for not coming earlier, but the tide was not right until the second half of the Hour of the Ox, and with the moon nearly full he thought I would prefer to go at night rather than wait for the afternoon tide. He seemed younger than the fisherman who'd sent him to me, and his speech was more refined and better educated, making him hard to place.

Makoto wanted to send at least one of the men with me, but my guide refused to take anyone else, saying his boat was too small. I offered to give him the silver before we left, but he laughed and said there was no point handing it over to the pirates so easily; he would take it when we returned, and if we did not return, someone else would come for it.

"If Lord Otori does not return, there will be no payment but the blade," Makoto said grimly.

"But if I die, my dependents deserve some compensation," he returned. "These are my conditions."

I agreed to them, overriding Makoto's misgivings. I wanted to get moving, to shake off the dread left by the dream. My horse, Shun, whickered to me as I left with the man. I'd charged Makoto to look after him with his life. I took Jato with me and, as usual, hidden under my clothes the weapons of the Tribe.

The boat was pulled up just above the high-water mark. We did not speak as we went to it. I helped him drag it into the water and jumped in. He pushed it farther out and then leaped in himself, sculling from the stern with the single oar. Later I took the oar while he hoisted a small square sail made of straw. It gleamed yellow in the moonlight, and amulets attached to the mast jingled in the offshore wind, which, together with the flow of the tide, would carry us to the island.

It was a brilliant night, the moon almost full throwing a silver track across the unruffled sea. The boat sang its song of wind and wave, the same song I remembered from the boats I'd been in with Fumio in Hagi. Something of the freedom and the illicit excitement of those nights came back to me now, dispelling the net of dread that the dream had caught me in.

Now I could see the young man standing at the end of the boat quite clearly. His features looked vaguely familiar; yet I did not think we had ever met before.

"What's your name?"

"Ryoma, sir."

"No other name?"

He shook his head and I thought he was not going to say any more. Well, he was taking me to Oshima; he did not have to talk to me as well. I yawned and pulled my robe closer round me. I thought I might as well sleep for a while.

Ryoma said, "If I had another name, it would be the same as yours."

My eyes snapped open and my hand went to Jato, for my first thought was that he meant Kikuta—that he was another of their assassins. But he did not move from the stern of the boat and went on calmly but with a trace of bitterness. "By rights I should be able to call myself Otori, but I have never been recognized by my father."

His story was a common enough one. His mother had been a maid at Hagi Castle, twenty years or so earlier. She had attracted the attention of the youngest Otori lord, Masahiro. When her pregnancy had been discovered, he claimed she was a prostitute and the child could be anyone's. Her family had no alternative but to sell her into prostitution; she became what she had been called and lost all chance of her son ever being recognized. Masahiro had plenty of legitimate sons and had no interest in any others.

"Yet people say I resemble him," he said. By now the stars had faded and the sky had paled. Day was breaking with a fiery sunrise as red as the previous night's sunset. I realized, now that I could see him properly, why he'd looked familiar. He had the Otori stamp on his features just as I did, marred like his father's by a slightly receding chin and cowed eyes.

"There is a likeness," I said. "So we are cousins."

I did not tell Ryoma, but I recalled all too clearly Masahiro's voice when I had overheard him say *If we were to adopt all our illegitimate children* . . . His son intrigued me; he was what I would have been but for the slightest divergences in our paths. I had been claimed by both sides of my ancestry, he by neither.

"And look at us," he said. "You are Lord Otori Takeo, adopted by Shigeru and rightful heir to the domain, and I am not much better than an outcast."

"You know something of my history, then?"

"My mother knows everything about the Otori," he said with a laugh. "Besides, you must know your own fame."

His manner was strange, ingratiating and familiar at the same time. I imagined his mother had spoiled him, bringing him up with unrealistic expectations and false ideas about his status, telling him stories about his relatives, the Otori lords, leaving him proud and dissatisfied, ill-equipped to deal with the reality of his life.

"Is that why you agreed to help me?"

"Partly. I wanted to meet you. I've worked for the Terada; I've been to Oshima many times. People call it the entrance to hell, but I've been there and survived." His voice sounded almost boastful, but when he spoke again it was with a note of pleading. "I hoped you might help me in return." He glanced at me. "Are you going to attack Hagi?"

I was not going to tell him too much in case he was a spy. "I think it's general knowledge that your father and his older brother betrayed Lord Shigeru to Iida. I hold them responsible for his death."

He grinned then. "That's what I hoped. I have a score to settle with them too."

"With your own father?"

"I hate him more than I would have thought it possible to hate any man," he replied. "The Terada hate the Otori too. If you move against them, you may find allies at Oshima."

This cousin of mine was no fool; he knew very well what my errand was. "I'm in your debt for taking me there," I said. "I've incurred many debts in seeking to avenge Shigeru's death fully, and when I hold Hagi I'll repay them all."

"Give me my name," he said. "That's all I want."

As we approached the island he told me how he went there from time to time, taking messages and snippets of information about expeditions to the mainland or shipments of silver, silk, and other precious goods between the coastal towns.

"The Terada can do no more than irritate the Otori," he said, "but between you maybe you can destroy them."

I neither agreed nor disagreed with him but tried to change the subject, asking him about the fisherman and how he came to know him.

"If you mean, do I believe the nonsense he does, the answer is no!" he said. He caught my look and laughed. "But my mother does. It's quite widespread among prostitutes. Perhaps it consoles them for their wretched lives. And besides, they should know if anyone does that all men are the same under their trappings. I don't believe in any god or any life beyond this one. No one's punished after death. That's why I want to see them punished now."

The sun had burned off the mist and the island's cone shape was now clearly visible, looming up out of the ocean, smoke rising from it. The waves broke white against the gray-black cliffs. The wind had strengthened and drove us skimming over the swell. The tidal race past the island quickened. I felt my stomach heave as we sped down the face of a huge green billow and up the other side. I stared upward toward the craggy island and took a couple of deep breaths. I did not want to be seasick when I faced the pirates.

Then we rounded the headland and came into the lee. Ryoma shouted to me to take the oar as the sail fluttered and sagged. He untied it and let it fall, then sculled the boat through the calmer water toward the sheltered port.

It was a natural deepwater harbor, with stone walls and breakwaters constructed around it. My heart lifted at the sight of the fleet of vessels moored there, ten or twelve at least, sturdy and seaworthy, capable of carrying dozens of men.

The port was guarded by wooden forts at each end, and I could see men inside at the arrow slits, bows no doubt trained on me. Ryoma waved and shouted, and two men emerged from the nearer fort. They did not wave back, but as they walked toward us one of them nodded perfunctorily in recognition.

As we approached the quayside he shouted, "Hey, Ryoma, who's the passenger?"

"Lord Otori Takeo," Ryoma called back importantly.

"Is that so? Your brother, is he? Another of your mother's mistakes?"

Ryoma took the boat up to the wharf skillfully enough and held it steady while I disembarked. The two men were still chuckling. I did not want to start a brawl, but I was not going to let them insult me and get away with it.

"I am Otori Takeo," I said. "No one's mistake. I am here to speak to Terada Fumio and his father."

"And we're here to keep people like you away from them," said the larger guard. His hair was long, his beard as thick as a northerner's, his face scarred. He waved his sword in my face and grinned. It was all too easy; his arrogance and stupidity made him immediately vulnerable to the Kikuta sleep. I held his gaze, his mouth dropped open, and his grin turned to a gasp of astonishment as his eyes rolled back and his knees buckled. He was a heavy man and he went down heavily, striking his head on the stones.

The other slashed out at me at once with his sword, but it was exactly the move I had expected and I'd already split myself and drawn Jato. As his sword went uselessly through my image, I struck it, twisted it, and sent it flying out of his hand.

"Please tell Terada I am here," I said.

Ryoma had fastened the boat and was on the quayside. He picked up the man's sword. "This is Lord Otori, you idiot. The one all the stories are about. You're lucky he didn't strike you dead on the spot."

Other men had come running from the fort. They all now dropped to their knees.

"Forgive me, lord. I didn't mean to offend you," the guard stammered, his eyes wide at what he no doubt thought was sorcery.

"Luckily for you I'm in a good mood," I said. "But you insulted my cousin. I think you should apologize to him."

With Jato pointed at his throat the man did so, causing Ryoma to smirk with satisfaction.

"What about Teruo?" the guard said, gesturing at his unconscious companion.

"He won't come to any harm. When he wakes up he'll have learned better manners. Now, be so good as to inform Terada Fumio of my arrival."

Two of them hurried away while the rest returned to the fort. I sat down on the quay wall. A tortoiseshell tomcat who had watched the whole encounter with interest came and sniffed at the recumbent man, then jumped onto the wall next to me and began to wash itself. It was the fattest cat I'd ever seen. Seafaring men are reputed to be superstitious; no doubt they believed the cat's coloring made it lucky, so they pampered it and fed it well. I wondered if they took it with them on their voyages.

I stroked the cat and looked around. Behind the port lay

a small village, and halfway up the hill behind it was a substantial wooden building, part house and part castle. It would have a fine view of the coast and the sea-lanes all the way to the city of Hagi. I couldn't help admiring the position and construction of the place and could understand why no one had been able to expel the pirates from their lair.

I saw the men hurry up the mountain path and heard their voices as they reported their message at the gates of the residence. Then I caught the familiar sound of Fumio's voice, a little deeper and more mature but with the same excited cadence that I remembered. I stood and walked to the end of the quay. The cat jumped down and followed me. By now quite a crowd had gathered, hostile and suspicious. I kept my hand near my sword and hoped the cat's presence would reassure them. They stood watching me curiously, most of them as tense as I was, while Ryoma kept them informed of my identity. "This is Lord Otori Takeo, Lord Shigeru's son and heir, who killed Iida." Every now and then he added, almost to himself, "He called me cousin."

Fumio came running down the hill. I'd been worried about my reception, but it was as warm as I could have hoped. We embraced like brothers. He looked older, had grown a mustache, and had filled out through the shoulders—in fact, he seemed as well fed as the cat—but his mobile face and lively eyes were unchanged.

"You came alone?" he asked, standing back and studying me.

"This man brought me." I indicated Ryoma, who had dropped to the ground at Fumio's approach. Whatever his pretensions, he knew where the real power lay. "I cannot stay long; I hope he will take me back again tonight."

"Wait here for Lord Otori," Fumio told him, and then as we began to walk away he called offhandedly to the guards, "Give him something to eat."

And don't tease him, I wanted to add, but was afraid of shaming him more. I hoped they would treat him better now but doubted it. He was the sort that invited ridicule, doomed always to be a victim.

"I imagine you've come for a purpose," Fumio said, striding up the hill. He'd lost none of his energy and stamina. "We'll bathe and eat, then I'll take you to my father."

No matter how urgent my mission, the lure of hot water was more pressing. The fortified house had been built around a string of pools where water bubbled from the rocks. Even without its violent inhabitants, Oshima, the entrance to hell, would have been a ferocious place. The volcano smoked above us, the air smelled of sulfur, and steam rose from the surface of the pools, where boulders loomed like the petrified dead.

We undressed and slid into the scalding water. I've never been in hotter. I thought my skin would be stripped from me. After the first agonizing moment the sensation was indescribable. It washed away the days of riding and sleeping rough, the nighttime boat trip. I knew I should be on my guard—a boyhood friendship was not much of a basis for trust—but at that moment anyone could have assassinated me and I would probably have died happy.

Fumio said, "We've had news of you from time to time. You have been busy since we last met. I was very sorry to hear of Lord Shigeru's death."

"It was a terrible loss, not only for me but for the clan. I am still pursuing his murderers."

"Iida is dead, though?"

"Yes, Iida has paid, but it was the Otori lords who planned Shigeru's death and who betrayed him to Iida."

"You intend to punish them? You can count on the Terada if you do."

I told him briefly about my marriage to Kaede, our journey to Maruyama, and the forces under our command.

"But I must return to Hagi and take up my inheritance there. The Otori lords will not give it to me peacefully, so I will take it from them by force. And I prefer it that way, for then I will destroy them too."

Fumio smiled and raised his eyebrows. "You have changed since I knew you first."

"I have been forced to."

We left the hot water, dressed, and were served food in one of the house's many rooms. It was like a storehouse, a treasure trove of valuable and beautiful objects, all presumably stolen from merchant ships: ivory carvings, celadon vases, brocade fabric, gold and silver bowls, tiger and leopard skins. I had never been in a room like it, so many precious things displayed but with none of the restraint and elegance that I was used to in the residences of the warrior class.

"Take a closer look at them," Fumio said when we'd finished eating. "I'll go and speak to my father. If there's anything that appeals to you, take it. My father acquires them, but they mean nothing to him."

I thanked him for the offer, but I had no intention of

taking anything back with me. I sat quietly waiting for his return, outwardly relaxed but on my guard. Fumio's welcome had been affectionate, but I had no idea what other alliances the Terada might have; for all I knew they might have an understanding with the Kikuta. I listened, placing everyone in the house, trying to identify voices, accents—though I had long since realized that if I was walking into a trap, I had little chance of escaping. I had truly come alone into the dragon's lair.

I had already placed Terada—the dragon himself— toward the back of the house. I'd heard his voice issuing orders, demanding tea, a fan, wine. The voice was rough, full of energy, like Fumio's, often passionate and also often angry, but sometimes revealing an underlying humor. I would not underestimate Terada Fumifusa. He had escaped the rigid hierarchy of the clan system, defied the Otori, and made his name one of the most feared in the Middle Country.

Finally, Fumio returned for me and led me to the back of the house, to a room like an eagle's nest, perched high above the village and the port, facing toward Hagi. In the distance I could just make out the familiar line of the ranges behind the town. The sea was still and calm, streaked like silk, indigo-colored, the waves forming a snowy fringe around the rocks. An eagle floated below, no bigger than a lark.

I had never been in a room like it. Even the top floor of the tallest castle was not this high or this open to the elements. I wondered what happened when the autumn typhoons came racing up the coast. The building was sheltered by the curve of the island; to construct something like this spoke of an immense pride as great as any warlord's.

Terada sat on a tiger skin facing the opened windows. Next to him on a low table were maps and charts, what looked like records of shipping, and a tube not unlike a bamboo flute. A scribe knelt at one end of the table, ink-stone in front of him, brush in hand.

I bowed low to Terada and spoke my name and parentage. He returned the bow, which was courteous, for if anyone held power in this place it was undoubtedly he.

"I have heard a lot about you from my son," he said. "You are welcome here." He gestured to me to come and sit at his side. As I moved forward, the scribe touched his head to the ground and stayed there.

"I hear you dropped one of my men without laying a finger on him. How did you do it?"

"He used to do it to dogs when we were boys," Fumio put in, sitting cross-legged on the floor.

"I have some talents like that," I said. "I did not want to hurt him."

"Tribe talents?" Terada demanded. I had no doubt he'd made use of them himself and knew perfectly well what they might be.

I inclined my head slightly.

His eyes narrowed and his lips pouted. "Show me what you do." He reached out and whacked the scribe on the head with his fan. "Do it to this man."

"Forgive me," I said. "Whatever small talents I have are not to be demonstrated as tricks."

"Unnh," he grunted, staring at me. "You mean you won't perform on demand?"

"Lord Terada has put it exactly."

There was a moment's uneasy silence, then he chuckled. "Fumio warned me I wouldn't be able to boss you around. You inherited more than the Otori look; you have their pig-headedness too. Well, I've not much use for magic—unless it's the sort that anyone can wield." He picked up the tube and placed its end against one eye, closing the other. "This is my magic," he said, and handed the tube to me. "What do you think of this?"

"Put it to your eye," Fumio said, grinning.

I held it gingerly, trying to sniff it unobtrusively in case it was poisoned.

Fumio laughed. "It's safe!"

I squinted through the tube and couldn't help gasping. The distant mountains, the town of Hagi, seemed to have leaped toward me. I took the tube away from my eye and they were back where they were before, hazy and indistinct. The Terada, father and son, were both chuckling now.

"What is it?" I said. It did not look or feel like something magic. It had been made by the hands of men.

"It's a sort of glass, carved like a lentil. It makes objects larger and brings the distant close," Terada said.

"Is it from the mainland?"

"We took it from a mainland ship and they have long had similar inventions there. But I believe this one was made in a distant country by the barbarians of the South." He leaned forward and took it from me, looked through it himself, and smiled. "Imagine countries and people who can make such things. We think we are the whole world here on the

Eight Islands, but sometimes I think we know nothing about anything."

"Men bring reports of weapons that kill from a huge distance with lead and fire," Fumio said. "We are trying to find some for ourselves." He gazed out of the window, his eyes filled with restless yearning for that vast world beyond. I imagined confinement to the island was like imprisonment to him.

Something about the strange artifact before me and the weapons of which he spoke filled me with a sense of foreboding. The height of the room, the sheer drop to the rocks below, my own tiredness, made my head reel for a moment. I tried to breathe deeply, calmly, but I could feel cold sweat break out on my forehead and prickle in my armpits. I foresaw that alliance with the pirates would both increase their strength and open the way to a flood of new things that would change completely the society I was struggling to establish myself in. The room had gone silent. I could hear the subdued sounds of the household around me, the beat of the eagle's wings, the distant hiss of the sea, the voices of the men at the port. A woman was singing quietly as she pounded rice, an old ballad of a girl who fell in love with a fisherman.

The air seemed to shimmer like the sea below, as though a veil of silk had been slowly withdrawn from the face of reality. Many months ago Kenji had told me that once all men had the skills that now only the Tribe retained—and among them only a handful of individuals like myself. Soon we would vanish, too, and our skills would be forgotten, overtaken by the technical magic that the Terada so desired. I thought of my own role in eradicating those skills, thought of the Tribe members I'd already destroyed, and felt a searing pang of regret. Yet I knew I was going to make a pact with the Terada. I would not recoil now. And if the far-seeing tube and the weapons of fire would help me, I would not hesitate to use them.

The room steadied. My blood flowed again. No more than a few moments had passed. Terada said, "I believe you have a proposal to make. I would be interested to hear it."

I told him I thought Hagi could only be taken from the sea. I outlined my plan to send half my army as a decoy to tie up the Otori forces on the riverbank while transporting the other half by ship and attacking the castle itself. In return for help from the Terada, I would reinstate them in Hagi and keep a permanent fleet of warships under their command.

Once peace was restored, the clan would finance expeditions to the mainland for the exchange of learning and trade.

"I know the strength and influence of your family," I concluded. "I cannot believe that you will stay here in Oshima forever."

"It is true that I would like to return to my family home," Terada replied. "The Otori confiscated it, as you know."

"It will be returned to you," I promised.

"You are very confident," he exclaimed, snorting with amusement.

"I know I can succeed with your help."

"When would you make this attack?"

Fumio glanced at me, his eyes bright.

"As soon as possible. Speed and surprise are among my greatest weapons."

"We expect the first typhoons any day now," Terada said. "That's why all our ships are in port. It will be over a month before we can put to sea again."

"Then we'll move as soon as the weather clears."

"You're no older than my son," he said. "What makes you think you can lead an army?"

I gave him details of our forces and equipment, our base

at Maruyama, and the battles we had already won. His eyes narrowed and he grunted, saying nothing for a while. I could read in him both caution and the desire for revenge. Finally he smacked his fan on the table, making the scribe flinch. He made a deep bow to me and spoke more formally than he had until now. "Lord Otori, I will help you in this endeavor and I'll see you instated in Hagi. The house and family of Terada swear it to you. We give you our allegiance, and our ships and men are yours to command."

I thanked him with some emotion. He had wine brought and we drank to our agreement. Fumio was elated; as I found out later, he had reasons of his own for wanting to return to Hagi, not least the girl he was to marry. The three of us ate the midday meal together, discussing troops and strategy. Toward the middle of the afternoon Fumio took me to the port to show me the ships.

Ryoma had been waiting on the quay, the tomcat sitting next to him. He greeted us effusively and followed me as closely as a shadow as we went on board the nearest ship and Fumio showed me around. I was impressed by its size and capacity and the way the pirates had fortified it with walls and shields of wood. It was fitted with huge canvas sails as well as many oars. The plan that had been a vague idea in my head suddenly became real.

We arranged that Fumio would send word to Ryoma as soon as the weather was favorable. I would begin moving my men north at the next full moon. The boats would come for us at the shrine, Katte Jinja, and would bring us to Oshima. We would make the assault on the city and the castle from there.

"Exploring Hagi at night—it'll be just like old times," Fumio said, grinning.

"I can't thank you enough. You must have pleaded my cause with your father."

"There was no need: He could see all the advantages of an alliance with you, and he recognizes you as the rightful heir to the clan. But I don't think he would have agreed if you had not come, in person, alone. He was impressed. He likes boldness."

I had known I must come in that fashion, but the knowledge weighed on me. So much to achieve, only I to achieve it, only I to hold together my patchy alliance.

Fumio wanted me to stay longer, but I was now more eager than ever to get back to Maruyama, to start preparations, to forestall at all costs an attack by Arai. Besides, I did not trust the weather. The air was unnaturally still and the sky had clouded over with a solid leaden color, black-tinged on the horizon.

Ryoma said, "If we leave soon we'll have the help of the tide again."

Fumio and I embraced on the quayside and I stepped down into the little boat. We waved farewell and cast off, letting the tide carry us away from the island.

Ryoma kept gazing anxiously at the leaden sky, and with reason, for we were barely half a mile from Oshima when the wind began to pick up. Within a few moments it was blowing hard, driving a stinging rain into our faces. We could make no headway against it with the oar, and as soon as we tried to put the sail up it was ripped from our hands.

Ryoma shouted, "We'll have to turn back."

I could not argue, though my spirits sank in despair at the thought of further delay. He managed to turn the fragile boat with the oar. The swell was getting heavier with every minute, great green waves that loomed above us and flung us upward only to drop us as if into a chasm. We must both have gone as green as the waves, and on the fourth or fifth drop we both vomited at the same time. The slight acrid smell seemed painfully feeble against the huge backdrop of wind and water.

The gale was blowing us toward the port, and we both struggled with the oar to guide the boat into the entrance. I did not think we would make it; I thought the force of the storm would drive us out into the open sea. But the sudden shelter in the lee of the land gave us a moment's grace to steer behind the breakwater. But even here we were not out of danger. The water inside the harbor was being churned like a boiling vat. Our boat was driven toward the wall, sucked back, and then thrown against it with a sickening smack.

It tipped over. I found myself struggling underwater, saw the surface above me, and tried to swim upward to it. Ryoma was a few feet from me. I saw his face, mouth open, as if he were calling for help. I caught hold of his clothes and dragged him up. We surfaced together. He took a great gasp of air and began to panic, flailing his arms and then grabbing me and almost strangling me. His weight took me underwater again. I could not free myself. I knew I could hold my breath for a long time, but sooner or later even I, with all my Tribe skills, had to breathe air. My head started to pound and my lungs ached. I tried to free myself from his grip, tried to reach his neck so I could disable him long enough to get us both out of this. I thought clearly, *He is my cousin, not my son,* and then, *Maybe the prophecy was wrong!*

I could not believe I was going to die by drowning. My vision was clouding, alternately black and filled with white light, and I felt an agonizing pain in my head.

I am being pulled into the next world, I thought, and then my face burst through the surface and I was taking great gulps of air.

Two of Fumio's men were in the water with us, attached by ropes to the quay. They had swum down to us and dragged us both up by the hair. They pulled us up onto the stones where we both vomited again, mostly seawater. Ryoma was in a worse state than I was. Like many sailors and fishermen, he did not know how to swim and had a terrible fear of drowning.

The rain was lashing down by now, completely obliterating the distant shore. The pirates' boats grunted and groaned as they were rocked together. Fumio was kneeling beside me.

"If you can walk now, we'll get inside before the worst of the storm."

I got to my feet. My throat ached and my eyes stung, but I was otherwise unhurt. I still had Jato in my belt, and my other weapons. There was nothing I could do against the weather, but I was filled with anger and anxiety.

"How long will it last?"

"I don't think it's a real typhoon, probably just a local storm. It could blow itself out by morning."

Fumio was too optimistic. The storm blew for three days, and for two more the seas were too heavy for Ryoma's little boat. It needed repairs anyway, which took four days to complete after the rain stopped. Fumio wanted to send me back in one of the pirates' ships, but I did not want to be seen in it or with them, fearing to reveal my strategy to spies. I spent the days restlessly, uneasy about Makoto—would he wait for me, would he return to Maruyama, would he abandon me altogether, now that he knew I was one of the Hidden, and go back to Terayama?—and even more anxious about Kaede. I had not meant to stay away from her for so long.

Fumio and I had the opportunity to have many conversations, about ships and navigation, fighting at sea, arming sailors, and so on. Followed everywhere by the tortoiseshell cat, who was as curious as I was, I inspected all the ships and weapons they had and was even more impressed by their power. And every night, while from below came the noise of the sailors gambling and their girls dancing and singing, we talked until late with his father. I came to appreciate even more the old man's shrewdness and courage, and I was glad he was going to be my ally.

The moon was past the last quarter when we finally set out on a calm sea in the late afternoon to take advantage of the evening tide. Ryoma had recovered from his near drowning and at my request had been received in the Terada residence on our last night and had eaten with us. The old pirate's presence had silenced him completely, but I knew he had felt the honor and been pleased by it.

There was enough wind to put up the new yellow canvas sail that the pirates had made for us. They had also given us fresh charms to replace the ones lost when the boat was damaged, as well as a small carving of the sea god, who they said obviously had us under his special protection. The charms sang in the wind, and as we sped past the southern side of the island there was a distant rumble like an echo, and a small gust of black smoke and ash rushed upward from the crater. The slopes of the island were shrouded in steam. I gazed at it for a long time, thinking the local people were right when they nicknamed it the entrance to hell. Gradually it dwindled and faded, until the lilac mist of evening came up off the sea and hid it completely.

We made the greater part of the crossing before nightfall, luckily, for the mist turned into solid cloud, and when darkness came it was complete. Ryoma alternated between bursts of chattiness and long, brooding silences. I could do little more than trust him and take turns with him at the oar. Long before the dark shape of the land loomed ahead of us, I'd heard the change in the note of the sea, the sucking of the waves on the shingle. We came ashore at the exact spot we had disembarked from, and Jiro was waiting on the beach next to a small fire. He leaped to his feet when the boat scraped on the stones, and held it while I jumped out.

"Lord Otori! We'd given up hope. Makoto was about to return to Maruyama to report you missing."

"We were delayed by the storm." I was filled with relief that they were still here, that they had not deserted me.

Ryoma was exhausted, but he did not want to leave the boat, nor would he rest till daylight. I guessed, despite his earlier boasting, he was afraid: He wanted to return to his home in the dark without anyone knowing where he'd been. I sent Jiro back to the shrine to fetch the silver we had promised him and whatever food we could spare. When we returned we would have to secure the coastline before we embarked, which would mean clearing it of bandits. I told Ryoma to expect us as soon as the weather settled.

He had become awkward again. I felt he wanted assurances and promises from me that I was not able to give. I thought I had disappointed him in some way. Perhaps he'd expected me to recognize him legally on the spot and take him with me to Maruyama, but I did not want to saddle myself with another dependent. On the other hand, I could not afford to antagonize him. I was relying on him as a messenger and I needed his silence. I tried to impress on him the necessity of utter secrecy, and hinted that his future status would depend on it. He swore he would tell no one and took the money and the food from Jiro with expressions of profound gratitude. I thanked him warmly—I was truly grateful to him—but I couldn't help feeling that an ordinary fisherman would have been easier to deal with and more trustworthy.

Makoto, deeply relieved at my safe return, had accompanied Jiro back down to the beach, and as we walked to the shrine I told him of the success of my journey, listening all the while to the faint splash of the oar as Ryoma rowed away in the darkness.

ACKNOWLEDGMENTS

I thank the Asialink Foundation, which awarded me a fellowship in 1999 to spend three months in Japan; the Australia Council, the Department of Foreign Affairs and Trade, and the Australian Embassy in Tokyo; and ArtsSA, the South Australian Government Arts Department. In Japan, I was sponsored by Yamaguchi Prefecture's Akiyoshidai International Arts Village, whose staff generously assisted me in exploring the landscape and the history of western Honshuu. Thanks particularly to Mr. Kori Yoshinori, Ms. Matsunaga Yayoi, and Ms. Matsubara Manami. I am especially grateful to Mrs. Tokoriki Masako for showing me the Sesshu paintings and gardens and to her husband, Professor Tokoriki, for information on horses in the medieval period.

Spending time in Japan with two theater companies gave me many insights. Deepest thanks to Kazenoko in Tokyo and Kyushuu, and Gekidan Urinko in Nagoya, and to Ms. Kimura Miyo, a wonderful traveling companion, who accompanied me to Kanazawa and the Nakasendo and who answered my questions about language and literature.

I am indebted to Mr. Morgi Masaru and Mrs. Mogi Akiko for their help with research, their suggestions for names, and above all, their ongoing friendship.

In Australia, I thank my two Japanese teachers, Mrs. Thuy Coombs and Mrs. Etsuko Wilson; Simon Higgins, who made invaluable suggestions; my agent, Jenny Darling; my son Matt, my first reader on all three books; and the rest of my family, for not only putting up with but also sharing my obsessions.

In 2002, I spent a further three months in Japan at the Shuho-cho Cultural Exchange House. Much of my research during this period was useful in the final rewriting of *Brilliance of the Moon*. My thanks to the people at Shuho-cho, in particular Ms. Santo Yuko and Mark Brachmann, and to Maxine McArthur. Also, again deepest thanks to ArtsSA for a Mid-Career Fellowship.

Calligraphy was drawn for me by Ms. Sugiyama Kazuko and Etsuko Wilson. I am immensely grateful to them.

TURN THE PAGE FOR A PREVIEW OF

Brilliance of the Moon

SCARS OF VICTORY

EPISODE
6

· *1* ·

When Takeo left for the coast, and the Miyoshi brothers for Inuyama, Kaede saw the excitement and anticipation on their faces and was filled with resentment at being left behind. In the days that followed she was plagued by fears and anxieties. She missed her husband's physical presence more than she would have thought possible; she was jealous of Makoto being allowed to accompany him when she was not; she feared for Takeo's safety and was angry with him at the same time.

His quest for revenge is more important to him than I am, she thought often. *Did he marry me just to further his plans of revenge?* She believed he loved her deeply, but he was a man, a warrior, and if he had to choose, she knew he would choose revenge. *I would be the same if I were a man,* she told herself. *I cannot even give him a child: What use am I as a woman? I should have been born a man. May I be allowed to return as one!*

She told no one of these thoughts. Indeed, there was no one in whom she could confide. Sugita and the other elders were polite, even affectionate, to her but seemed to avoid her company. She kept herself busy all day, overseeing the household, riding out with Amano, and making copies of the records that Takeo had entrusted to her. After the attempted theft she'd thought it would be a wise precaution and she hoped it would help her understand the ferocity of Takeo's campaign against the Tribe and the anguish it had caused him. She herself had been disturbed by the slaughter, and also by the piles of dead after the battle at Asagawa. It took so long to raise a man, and life was extinguished so easily. She feared retribution, both from the living and from the dead. Yet what else could Takeo do when so many were conspiring to kill him?

She, too, had killed, had had men killed on her orders: Had losing her child been punishment for her own actions? Her desires were changing; now she was moved to protect and to nurture, to create life, not to destroy it. Was it possible to hold on to her domain and rule it without violence? She had many hours of solitude to think about these things.

Takeo had said he would be back within a week; the time passed, he did not return, and her anxiety grew. There were plans and decisions that needed to be made about the domain's future, but the elders continued to be evasive, and every suggestion she made to Sugita was greeted by a deep bow and the advice to wait until her husband returned. Twice she tried to summon the elders for a council meeting, but one by one they pleaded indisposition.

"It's remarkable that everyone is sick on the same day," she said tartly to Sugita. "I had no idea that Maruyama was so unhealthy for old people."

"Be patient, Lady Kaede," he said. "Nothing needs to be decided before Lord Takeo's return, and that will be any day now. He may have urgent commands for the men; they must be kept in readiness for him. All we can do is wait for him."

Her irritation was compounded by the realization that, even though it was her domain, everyone still deferred to Takeo. He was her husband and she must defer to him, too; yet Maruyama and Shirakawa were hers and she should be

3

able to act in them as she wished. Part of her was shocked that Takeo had gone to make an alliance with pirates. It was like his association with outcasts and farmers: There was something unnatural about it. She thought it must all come from being born into the Hidden. This knowledge that he had shared with her both attracted and repelled her. All the rules of her class told her that her blood was purer than his and that by birth she was of higher rank. She was ashamed of this feeling and tried to suppress it, but it niggled at her and the longer he was away, the more insistent it became.

"Where is your nephew?" she said to Sugita, wanting distraction. "Send him to me. Let me look at someone under the age of thirty!"

Hiroshi was hardly better company, equally resentful at being left behind. He had hoped to go to Inuyama with Kahei and Gemba.

"They don't even know the road," he grumbled. "I would have shown them everything. I have to stay here and study with my uncle. Even Jiro was allowed to go with Lord Otori."

"Jiro is much older than you," Kaede said.

"Only five years. And he's the one who should be studying. I already know far more letters than he does."

4

"That's because you started earlier. You should never despise people because they haven't had your opportunities." She studied him; he was a little small for his age, but strong and well put together; he would be a handsome man. "You are about the same age as my sister," she said.

"Does your sister look like you?"

"People say so. I think she is more beautiful."

"That couldn't be possible," he said quickly, making her laugh. His face colored slightly. "Everyone says Lady Otori is the most beautiful woman in the Three Countries."

"What have they seen?" she retorted. "In the capital, in the emperor's court, there are women so lovely men's eyes shrivel up when they look at them. They are kept behind screens lest the whole court go blind."

"What do their husbands do?" he said doubtfully.

"They have to wear blindfolds," she teased, and threw a cloth that lay next to her over his head. She held him playfully for a few moments, then he twisted away from her. She saw he was ruffled; she had treated him like a child and he wanted to be a man.

"Girls are lucky: They don't have to study," he said.

"But my sister loves to study and so do I. Girls should

learn to read and write just the same as boys. Then they can help their husbands, as I am helping mine."

"Most people have scribes to do that sort of thing, especially if they can't write themselves."

"My husband can write," she said swiftly, "but like Jiro he started learning later than you."

Hiroshi looked horrified. "I didn't mean to say anything against him! Lord Otori saved my life and revenged my father's death. I owe everything to him, but . . ."

"But what?" she prompted, uncomfortably aware of some shadow of disloyalty.

"I'm only telling you what people say," Hiroshi said. "They say he is strange. He mixes with outcasts; he lets farmers fight; he has started a campaign against certain merchants that no one understands. They say he cannot have been brought up as a warrior, and they wonder what his upbringing was."

"Who says it? The townspeople?"

"No, people like my family."

"Maruyama warriors?"

"Yes, and some say he is a sorcerer."

She could hardly be surprised; these were exactly the

things that worried her about Takeo; yet she was outraged that her warriors should be so disloyal to him.

"Maybe his upbringing was a little unusual," she said, "but he is heir to the Otori clan by blood and by adoption, as well as being my husband. No one has the right to say anything against him." She would find out who it was and have them silenced. "You must be my spy," she said to Hiroshi. "Report to me anyone who gives the slightest sign of disloyalty."

After that, Hiroshi came to her every day, showed her what he had learned in his studies, and told her what he heard among the warrior class. It was nothing definite, just whispers, sometimes jokes, maybe no more than the idle chatter of men with not enough to occupy themselves. She resolved to do nothing about it for the time being but to warn Takeo when he returned.

The time of the great heat began, and it was too sultry to ride outside. Since Kaede could take no decisions till Takeo's return, and since she expected him every day, she spent most of her time kneeling at the lacquer writing table, copying the Tribe records. The doors to the residence were all opened to catch the least breeze, and the sound of insects was deafening. Her preferred room looked out over pools and a waterfall; through the azalea bushes she could see the silver-weathered tea house. Every day she promised herself that she would make tea there for Takeo that night, and every day she was disappointed. Sometimes kingfishers came to the pools and the flash of blue and orange would distract her momentarily. Once a heron alighted outside the veranda and she thought it was a sign that he would be back that day, but he did not come.

She let no one see what she was writing, for she quickly realized the importance of the records. She was amazed at what Shigeru had uncovered, and wondered if someone within the Tribe had acted as his informant. She concealed the original records and the copies in a different place every night and tried to commit as much as possible to memory. She became obsessed with the idea of the secret network, watched for signs of them everywhere, trusted no one, even though Takeo's first work at Maruyama had been to purge the castle household. The range of the Tribe daunted her; she did not see how Takeo would ever escape them. Then the thought would come to her that they had already caught up with him—that he was lying dead somewhere and she would never see him again.

He was right, she thought. *They must all be killed; they must be rooted out, for they seek to destroy him. And if they destroy him, they destroy me.*

The faces of Shizuka and Muto Kenji often rose before her mind's eye. She regretted the trust she had placed in Shizuka and wondered how much of Kaede's life her companion had revealed to others in the Tribe. She had thought that both Shizuka and Kenji had been fond of her; had all that affection been feigned? They had nearly died together in Inuyama Castle; did that count for nothing? She felt betrayed by Shizuka, but at the same time she missed her badly and wished she had someone like her to confide in.

Her monthly bleeding came, bringing her renewed disappointment and placing her in seclusion for a week. Not even Hiroshi visited her. When it was over the copying was finished, too, and she became even more restless. The Festival of the Dead came and went, leaving her filled with sorrow and regrets for the departed. The work on the residence that had gone on all summer was completed, and the rooms looked beautiful, but they felt empty and unlived in. Hiroshi asked one morning, "Why isn't your sister here with you?" and on a sudden impulse she said, "Shall we ride to my house and fetch her?"

9

There had been a week of leaden skies, as if a typhoon were threatening, but then the weather had suddenly cleared and the heat had abated a little. The nights were cooler and it seemed a perfect time to travel. Sugita tried to dissuade her, and even the elusive elders appeared one by one to argue against it, but she ignored them. Shirakawa was only two or three days away. If Takeo came home before she returned, he might ride and join her. And the journey would stop her from fretting all day long.

"We can send for your sisters," Sugita said. "It is an excellent idea; I should have thought of it myself. I will go to escort them."

"I need to see my household," she replied. Now that the idea was in her head, she could not relinquish it. "I have not spoken to my men since my marriage. I should have gone weeks ago. I must check on my land and see that the harvest will be brought in."

She did not tell Sugita, but she had another reason for the journey, one that had lain in her mind all summer. She would go to the sacred caves of the Shirakawa, drink the river's elemental water, and pray to the goddess for a child.

"I will be away only a few days."

"I am afraid your husband will not approve."

"He trusts my judgment in all things," she replied. "And, after all, didn't Lady Naomi often travel alone?"

Because he was accustomed to receiving orders from a woman, she was able to overcome his misgivings. She chose Amano to go with her, as well as a few of her own men who had accompanied her since she had left in the spring for Terayama. After some consideration she took none of her women with her, not even Manami. She wanted to go quickly, on horseback, without the formalities and dignity that she would have to put up with if she traveled openly. Manami pleaded and then sulked, but Kaede was adamant.

She rode Raku, refusing even to take a palanquin with her. Before she left she had planned to hide the copies of the records below the floor of the tea room, but the hints of disloyalty still worried her, and in the end she could not bear to leave them where anyone might find them. She decided to take both sets with her, already thinking she might hide the originals somewhere in her house at Shirakawa. After much pleading, Hiroshi was allowed to accompany her, and she took him to one side and made him promise not to let the chests out of his sight on the journey. And at the last moment she took the sword Takeo had given her.

Amano managed to persuade Hiroshi to leave his father's sword behind, but the boy brought a dagger and his bow as well as a small, fiery roan horse from his family's stables that acted up all the first day, causing the men endless amusement. Twice it wheeled round and bolted, heading for home, until the boy brought it under control and caught up with them, blue-faced with rage but otherwise undaunted.

"He's a nice-looking creature, but green," Amano said. "And you make him tense. Don't grip so hard. Relax."

He made Hiroshi ride alongside him; the horse settled down and the next day gave no problems. Kaede was happy to be on the road. As she had hoped, it kept her from brooding. The weather was fine, the country in the full flush of harvest, the men cheerful at the prospect of seeing their homes and families after months away. Hiroshi was a good companion, full of information about the land they passed through.

"I wish my father had taught me as much as yours taught you," she said, impressed by his knowledge. "When I was your age I was a hostage in Noguchi Castle."

"He made me learn all the time. He would not allow me to waste a moment."

"Life is so short and fragile," Kaede said. "Perhaps he knew he would not see you grow up."

Hiroshi nodded and rode in silence for a while.

He must miss his father, but he will not show it, she thought, and found herself envying the way he had been taught. *I will have my children brought up that way; girls as well as boys will be taught everything and will learn to be strong.*

On the morning of the third day they crossed the Shirakawa, or White River, and entered her family's domain. It was shallow and easily fordable, the swift white water swirling between rocks. There was no barrier at the border; they were beyond the jurisdiction of the great clans and in the region of smaller landholders, where neighbors either were involved in petty standoffs or had formed amicable alliances among themselves. Nominally these warrior families paid allegiance to Kumamoto or Maruyama, but they did not move to the castle towns, preferring to live on and farm their own lands, on which they paid very little tax to anyone.

"I've never crossed the Shirakawa before," Hiroshi said as

the horses splashed through. "This is the farthest I've been from Maruyama."

"So now it's my turn to instruct you," she said, taking pleasure in pointing out the landmarks of her country. "I will take you to the source of the river later, to the great caves, only you will have to wait outside."

"Why?" he demanded.

"It's a sacred place for women. No men are allowed to set foot in there."

She was eager to get home now and they did not linger on the way, but she was studying everything: the look of the land, the progress of the harvest, the condition of oxen and children. Compared to a year ago when she had returned with Shizuka, things had improved, but there were still many signs of poverty and neglect.

I abandoned them, she thought guiltily. *I should have come home before.* She thought of her tempestuous flight to Terayama in the spring: She seemed to have been another person, bewitched.

Amano had sent two of the men ahead, and Shoji Kiyoshi, the domain's senior retainer, was waiting for her at the gate of her house. He greeted her with surprise and, she thought, coolness. The household women were lined up in the garden, but there was no sign of her sisters or Ayame.

Raku whinnied, turning his head toward the stables and the water meadows where he had run in the winter. Amano came forward to help her dismount. Hiroshi slid from the roan's back and it tried to kick the horse next to it.

"Where are my sisters?" Kaede demanded, brushing aside the women's murmured greetings.

No one answered. A shrike was calling insistently from the camphor tree by the gate, grating on her nerves.

"Lady Shirakawa . . ." Shoji began.

She spun to face him. "Where are they?"

"We were told . . . you sent instructions for them to go to Lord Fujiwara."

"I did no such thing! How long have they been there?"

"Two months at least." He glanced at the horsemen and the servants. "We should speak in private."

"Yes, at once," she agreed.

One of the women ran forward with a bowl of water.

"Welcome home, Lady Shirakawa."

Kaede washed her feet and stepped onto the veranda. Unease was beginning to creep through her. The house was eerily quiet. She wanted to hear Hana's and Ai's voices; she realized how much she had missed them.

It was a little after noon. She gave instructions for the men to be fed, the horses watered, and both to be kept ready in case she needed them. She took Hiroshi to her own room and told him to stay there with the records while she spoke to Shoji. She was not hungry at all, but she arranged for the women to bring food to the boy. Then she went to her father's old room and sent for Shoji.

The room looked as if someone had just walked out of it. There was a brush lying on the writing table. Hana must have gone on with her studies even after Kaede's departure. She picked up the brush and was staring at it dully when Shoji tapped on the door.

He entered and knelt before her, apologizing. "We had no idea it was not your wish. It seemed so likely. Lord Fujiwara himself came and spoke to Ai."

She thought she detected insincerity in his voice. "Why did he invite them? What did he want with them?" Her voice was trembling.

"You yourself often went there," Shoji replied.

"Everything has changed since then!" she exclaimed.

"Lord Otori Takeo and I were married at Terayama. We have established ourselves at Maruyama. You must have heard of this."

"I found it hard to believe," he replied, "since everyone thought you were betrothed to Lord Fujiwara and were to marry him."

"There was no betrothal!" she said in fury. "How dare you question my marriage!"

She saw the muscles round his jaw tense and realized he was as angry as she was. He leaned forward. "What are we to think?" he hissed. "We hear of a marriage that is undertaken with no betrothal, no permission asked or given, none of your family present. I am glad your father is already dead. You killed him by the shame you brought on him, but at least he is spared this fresh shame—"

He broke off. They stared at each other, both shocked by his outburst.

I'll have to take his life, Kaede thought in horror. *He cannot speak to me like that and live. But I need him: Who else can look after things here for me?* Then the fear came to her that he might try and take the domain from her, using his anger to mask ambition and greed. She wondered if he had taken control of the men she and Kondo had gathered together in the winter—and if they would obey him now. She wished Kondo were there, then realized that she could trust the Tribe man even less than her father's senior retainer. No one could help her. Struggling to hide her apprehension, she continued to stare at Shoji until he lowered his eyes.

He regained control of himself, wiping the spittle from his mouth. "Forgive me. I have known you since you were born. It is my duty to speak to you, even though it pains me."

"I will forgive you this time," she said. "But it is you who shame my father, through disrespect to his heir. If you ever speak to me in that fashion again, I will order you to slit your belly."

"You are only a woman," he said, trying to placate her but enraging her further. "You have no one to guide you."

"I have my husband," she said shortly. "There is nothing you or Lord Fujiwara can do to alter that. Go to him now and say my sisters are to come home at once. They will return with me to Maruyama."

He left immediately. Shocked and restless, she could not sit quietly and wait for his return. She called to Hiroshi and showed him the house and garden while she checked all the repairs that she had had done in the autumn. The crested ibis in their summer plumage were feeding on the banks of the rice fields, and the shrike continued to scold them as they trespassed into its territory. Then she told him to fetch the chests of records and, carrying one each, they made their way upstream along the Shirakawa to where it emerged from under the mountain. She would not hide them where Shoji might find them; she would entrust them to no human. She had decided to give them to the goddess.

The holy place calmed her, as always, but its ageless, sacred atmosphere awed her rather than lifted her spirits. Below the huge arch of the cave's entrance the river flowed slowly and steadily in deep pools of green water, belying its name, and the twisted shapes of the calcified rocks gleamed like mother-of-pearl in the half-light.

The old couple who maintained the shrine came out to greet her. Leaving Hiroshi in the company of the man, Kaede went forward with his wife, each of them carrying one of the chests.

Lamps and candles had been lit inside the cavern, and the damp rock glistened. The roar of the river drowned out all other noise. They stepped carefully from stone to stone, past the giant mushroom, past the frozen waterfall, past Heaven's Stairway—all shapes made by the limy water—until they came to the rock shaped like the goddess, from which drops fell like tears of mother's milk.

Kaede said, "I must ask the goddess to protect these treasures for me. Unless I myself come for them, they must stay here with her forever."

The old woman nodded and bowed. Behind the rock a cave had been hollowed out, well above the highest level of the river. They climbed up to it and placed the chests in it. Kaede noticed that it contained many other objects that had been given to the goddess. She wondered about their history and what had happened to the women who had placed them there. There was a damp, ancient smell. Some of the objects were decaying; some had already rotted. Would the records of the Tribe rot away there, hidden under the mountain?

The air was cold and clammy, making her shiver. When she put the chest down, her arms felt suddenly empty and light. She was seized by the knowledge that the goddess knew her need—that her empty arms, her empty womb, would be filled.